A Tempting Trio

Bettina Hunt

Copyright © 2015 Bettina Hunt

All rights reserved.

ISBN: 1534917845
ISBN-13: 978-1534917842

DEDICATION

This book is dedicated to my parents who always taught me
to believe, to follow my dreams and never give up.

PROLOGUE

'Would you like to see the dessert menu?

The beaming waitress stood in anticipation with the menu already in her hand... Sarah was really rather full after the main course but somehow the mere suggestion ignited her other belly, you know the one that we all possess - the pudding one, and so she found herself saying yes please.

Banoffee Pie

Chocolate Fudge Cake

Eton Mess

Sarah glanced down at the menu and considered the options on offer, she loved food but dessert was where her heart truly belonged. What a wonderful selection, all were tempting her but she had narrowed down her choices. Truth be known she was secretly marvelling at how she could quite easily devour all three without a second thought but making up her mind was the hardest part, working her way down the menu she cried out in triumph.

'Having trouble choosing? Why not enjoy a trio of our tempting desserts - a smaller portion of each of our most popular desserts'

Wow that was easy! Decision made, she ordered her dessert. She may have, for a fleeting moment, felt a bit greedy but this feeling dispersed as soon as the plate was placed in front of her.

Sarah found her mind drifting and with each delicious mouthful she weighed up the pros and cons of each of them.

Banoffee Pie

Adam - Devilishly handsome with dreamy blue eyes. A soft and squidgy exterior, but well defined with a caring sweetness that made her melt every time they met and yet, there was this hard core that she couldn't penetrate that made her feel that Adam was holding back.

Adam was complicated and gave nothing away. Each time they met she unpeeled another layer and found out something new but all the pieces just didn't add up. Dates were carefully planned and each one was accompanied by a gift. Adam was sweet, generous and loving but there was something missing.

Sarah sighed...mmm I am not quite ready to give it up, I need to find out what is stopping Adam committing to me completely. I don't just want a piece, it is just not enough, I want it all.

The fact that Adam may know about the others and that was why he was reluctant to give his all never even entered Sarah's head.

Irresistible Adam, the mysterious one.

Chocolate Fudge Cake

David - Ah David... If Adam had dreamy blue eyes, David had the most deliciously big brown eyes she had ever seen. He with his glossy exterior but who was warm and well she couldn't deny it, rich. He reached right down to the very heart of her soul. Taking her to places she could only dream of. Unfortunately he was also married which should have set alarm bells ringing but it was true he was trying to extricate himself from his wife but it was going to take time.

Could she wait, were the trips to St Tropez enough to placate her? Were the shopping trips to Selfridges and the open wallet enough, even if come the weekend she was left twiddling her thumbs? Sarah thought hard, really hard. He did LOVE her, they had just found each other at the wrong time.

Neither of them were superficial, her thoughts made it sound like she was and that he could buy her submission but actually when they were together they loved nothing better than the ordinary things in life, like opening a tub of ice cream and tucking in whilst watching videos and laughing to their heart's content.

Sarah laughed aloud and then quickly remembered where she was. She looked around and hoped no-one had noticed her. Embarrassed she started on her last dessert. Tucking into oodles of meringue pieces, cream and strawberries, Sarah's mind once again began to wander.

Eton Mess

Tommy - Finally Tommy, the foppish and incredibly sexy aristocrat who was fruity if a little fresh at times. Time spent with him was a blur. He was unreliable, dishevelled and unshaven. Stuck in the 90's he still had curtain hair for god's sake and his dress sense was terrible. But and there was a huge but he was so much fun to be around, if and when he turned up.

He embraced culture like it was going out of fashion, showing Sarah the beauty of the museum, since they had 'dated' they had been to them all. Her favourite was the V&A, especially the great exhibitions and showcases. Tommy let her be a dreamer, actively encouraged her in fact. She swirled around with fabrics and they giggled as people stared. Tommy loved the art galleries, they would sit and gaze for hours at each individual brush stroke and then people watch. Tommy mimicking mannerisms and she adoring his little quirks.

However, life she could tell with Tommy would be messy, the room in his stately home a tip. He called it organized chaos but she knew he was a hoarder and she was such a tidy person. She loved to plan, he loved surprises and last minute activities.

Could she see past the cons with Tommy and indulge in an alternative lifestyle?

Decisions, decisions. A tempting trio indeed, she just couldn't make her mind up. Why wasn't life as simple as the dessert menu?

CHAPTER ONE

Life was getting far too complicated that was for sure and Sarah Dawes wasn't certain she could keep up this duplicitous life for much longer, there was only one thing for it she HAD to make up her mind once and for all.

Two years ago she had thought that she would never get a decent boyfriend and then, like buses, three eligible bachelors came along at once.

David, although strictly not a bachelor was a predictable conquest from the office, he of the older man variety and she as his equally predictable personal assistant. If she had intended it to be a one off office party bonk, she soon found out that David had quite different ideas. The next morning he had turned up to the office with a huge and beautiful bunch of red roses with a promise of a dinner date and it had just gone on from there. It seemed like he didn't need any excuse to regularly escape that stuck up bitch of a wife Laura and yet two years down the line it was she that he was returning home to night after night.

David as her boss pretty much left her to her own devices which suited her just fine until the day that his boss decided to give her an appraisal, found she didn't actually do any work bar the odd letter for David and promptly dismissed her.

Stirring her coffee in Starbucks an hour later, clockwise and then anticlockwise with no particular purpose she barely noticed the gorgeous azure eyes of the kindly face that was standing over her. 'Penny for your thoughts?'

'Hmmm?' she said still miles away until she finally looked up and had to do a double take as there stood in front of her was the handsomest man she had ever seen. Super smooth and chiselled he could have walked straight out of a Next catalogue shoot, he probably had Sarah thought, what on earth was he doing here with her.

'You look so sad, want to chat? May I sit here?' Sarah looked around there were no tables free, of course he wasn't interested in her, he just wanted a chair to plonk his bottom down on. She should have known!

Still it wouldn't hurt her reputation to be seen to have this delicious man sat down with her, so taking pity on him she moved her bag so he could sit down.

Actually, she wasn't really in the mood for making small talk with a stranger, to just to sit and stare at him would be just fine. Except she could feel her eyes welling up with tears, pull yourself together Sarah she thought to herself, only it turned out that she hadn't thought it at all.

'What?' Oh crap had she said that out loud.

'Oh nothing!'

'The tears falling down your cheeks are not nothing lady, talk to me, I am a good listener.'

Oh his voice, who was this Guardian Angel sent from above, something made her want to pour out her heart and tell him everything but she didn't even know his name. Perhaps it was better this way, she could treat him a bit like a counsellor, only she wouldn't have to see him again…

As she opened her mouth to say something her words were drowned out by the Frappuccino machine, oh typical this obviously wasn't meant to be.

He yelled 'Sorry, what? I can't hear you!'

'Never mind,' she mouthed and then laughed. This was ridiculous.

As things quietened down again he laughed too 'Not really romantic is it, I mean IF you were on a date?'

'I could think of better dates,' Sarah quipped.

'Yes of course,' his face fell 'Oh by the way, my name is Adam.'

'Sarah.'

'Nice to meet you, I have to get going now I am afraid.' Sarah watched Adam scribble something on a napkin and in a flash he was gone.

Left on the table was a plate of Panini crumbs, a half drunken Latte and the napkin, glancing down she saw a mobile number on it with the words 'Call Me x'

'As if!' She thought and left it on the table and walked out of the door. As she walked down the street she suddenly had a change of heart, they did say people walked into your life for a reason. She HAD to get that number back!! She ran back, panting heavily, she was not used to exercising, with all the energy she could muster she pushed the door open and flopped into the coffee shop. Her heart sank, there were people at the table that minutes before they had been sat at. She rushed over to them and oh thank god, the staff had been rubbish at clearing the table, there was the note! Snatching it off the table and ignoring the bemused looks from the people at the table she held it close to her chest.

She popped the number into her phone and threw the napkin in the bin.

Maybe life was about to improve. She went home, updated her CV, hesitating to put David as a reference but if anyone knew her best it was him. Inside and out.

Her phone beeped with a text message, for a moment her heart lurched, Adam had texted her and then she remembered that he couldn't have as she hadn't given him her number. It was a message from David.

'I am so sorry, please meet me for dinner tomorrow x'

CHAPTER TWO

Sarah sat in Pizza Express waiting for David to arrive, usually she would be the one to turn up late, the one who would make the grand entrance but this was only Pizza Express after all. An odd choice from David but this particular branches feature was that it had a Jazz Evening. Asking the waitress for a glass of white wine she looked around and people watched. She loved imagining what conversations the other people were having and then it suddenly dawned on her why David had chosen Pizza Express, he was going to dump her!

She had read an article a while back in the newspaper about some research that found that Pizza Express was the top choice for people wanting to dump their other half. Oh marvellous, she would save him the bother, she was going to leave before he arrived. How dare he? Just who did he think he was? He may have the money but she still had her dignity. She swigged back the glass of wine, well it would be a shame to waste it! Stood up to leave only to see David coming through the double doors. Too late, she looked around and contemplated leaving through a toilet window but decided against it based on the outfit she was wearing.

Defeated she sat back down.

'Sarah darling, I am sorry I am late, Dan called a late meeting that I had no option but to attend.'

'Dan or your wife?'

'Sarah, don't be silly.'

'David save it. I know why we are here so I am going to save you the time and effort. Goodbye!'

'What on earth are you on about, what are you saying? Are you leaving me?'

'That's the plan, it IS what you wanted.'

'What? No! I love you Sarah, whatever gave you that idea?'

'Pizza Express, a lover's dumping ground... you, me here.'

'Eh? God no! I thought it would be nice to listen to a bit of Jazz, work is so hectic without you being around to help, I just wanted to relax.'

'Oh…I am such an idiot and really David you know I didn't do much in the office.'

'Well I miss you,' he grinned.

Sarah relaxed, she did feel like an idiot and called the waitress over, this time ordering a bottle of wine.

By the time they left Pizza Express she felt a bit squiffy and all warm and glowy inside, she had David's sole attention and adulation. With his strong arms holding her upright and steady, all thoughts of anything else had quite frankly left the building.

As was customary they went back to her flat, and quickly fell into the bedroom. This time however it felt different. David was all hers in body and mind, a night when two became one. This really was true love she thought.

Next morning however was a different story, if last night she had imagined waking up entwined in his arms the reality was nothing of the kind. To the sound of her alarm getting louder and louder (she swore it was the most aggressive alarm in the world) she woke with a start, looked around to find David had clearly upped and left early. Her head hurt and she still felt drowsy, damn that bottle of wine! Her head flopped back onto the pillow and she drifted back off to sleep again, not to nice dreams though. David's wife was banging on her flat door, screaming 'Give me back my husband!'

The next time Sarah woke it was midday and someone was banging on her door 'Oh shit, David's wife!' Sarah pulled on her rabbit onesie, it was the first thing to hand, and rushed to the door.

'Alice,' she sighed with relief.

'Nice outfit Sarah.'

'Oh shut up, I feel like crap.'

'Are you OK? You were supposed to meet me at 10am, I tried calling you on the moby but got no answer, I was worried about you.'

'Oh god, I am SO sorry. I was out with David last night, drank too much and fell back to sleep this morning.'

'Sarah, I have been thinking about this, we should probably forget about being business partners right now.'

'What? No. I can be reliable I PROMISE, it is just that I thought David was going to break up with me and when I found out he wasn't I got a bit too wine happy. I want to work in event planning with you more than anything. You are my best friend and I know this is going to work, truly.'

'Sarah I know you just want to work with me until you get another job but honestly, if you mess up, you are out. Do you understand? People rely on me to supply the best parties and events. You need to be 100% committed too.'

'Alice, look I know what you think but I really do fancy a change of career and I know for our first meeting I let you down but it won't ever, ever, happen again. Promise.'

Alice had been running an events planning business quite successfully alone for a few years now but as it was growing at a pace she was finding hard to keep up with, thought it time to bring in a partner. She had known Sarah since their University days and knew she was exceptional in her organisational skills, Sarah had been Student Union President taking her responsibility very seriously. Though now it seemed their roles had changed. Alice was professional and serious when it came to her business and Sarah, well Sarah had been an excellent PA but her career although on paper had flourished the reality was she had done very little of value since leaving University.

Alice made her way into the kitchen and made them both a cup of sweet tea. Sarah had changed into a comfy pair of jeans and a t shirt. How could she possibly have a serious business chat dressed in a ridiculous onesie.

Alice passed Sarah brief notes on the latest event they were set to plan, a society guy had asked her for a party in a castle, the theme being Count Dracula. Sarah smiled, oh she could really go to town with this theme, she was thinking lots of fake blood and fabulous costumed serving staff, a few oddball actors to randomly scare the guests and of course incredible ghoulish food and drink. Then she saw the budget for the party and nearly choked on her tea.

'How much?!!'

'I know! This guy is loaded Sarah, if this is pulled off this is going to be the best party ever for 'Perfect Events' I cannot wait to put this in my portfolio, this has the potential to make my business go through the roof! Once word gets around, everyone who's who will want my services.'

'Oh Alice, I am SO happy for you.'

'Sarah it is going to take a lot of hard work and is going to need plenty of client liaison, rumour has it that he is a fussy bugger but willing to pay for the best, so we have to recruit the very best and not cut corners. I am so excited, I will handle all the big things but day to day I want you to speak with him, smooth things over and make sure the plans are running to schedule. Do you think you can handle it?'

'Alice, you have my word.'

'Great, I am relying on you!'

They clinked their teacups together and laughed.

CHAPTER THREE

Next morning Sarah was up bright and early, singing in the shower at the top of her voice 'Working 9-5 what a way to make a living La la la.' She straightened her hair (her naturally wild, wavy hair always seemed less professional than when it was poker straight), dusted down her long neglected power suit and put on her stiletto ankle straps that always managed to make her feel all powerful inside.

She was back on the daily commute and feeling pretty pleased. The tube was packed as ever but there was something satisfying about being back on the grind waggon. She looked at the other passengers on the train, no one was smiling, some were grimacing and others were just staring down at their iPad or phones. Failing to make eye contact with anyone, Sarah decided to pop in her earphones and listen to some uplifting music to make the journey pass quicker.

She headed to Alice's office, a rented large room in an

office block on Old Street, buzzed herself in and waited for Alice in reception. Alice walked in moments behind her.

'Wow, Sarah I am impressed!'

'Start as you mean to go on Alice that is my motto.'

Alice opened up the office, it was a bit bare but functional. Sarah had a quick scan around and noted the whereabouts of the toilet and kitchen, the daily essentials as she called them.

'Shall I make us a coffee Alice?'

'Ooh yes please, then join me for a quick tour of the office and your equipment.'

'Two coffee lattes coming right up.'

Sipping her coffee brought back memories of her encounter with Adam, she hadn't done anything with his phone number and she was still weighing up whether she even should. Things were going quite nicely with David, she was about to be busy with her new job and life was generally ok, she didn't need any complications. It would be so easy to just forget about him but those blue eyes, she smiled to herself. She didn't need him in her life but he seemed quite nice, maybe they could just go for a drink, it would be a chance to get dressed up and have a little fun. Not a date as such, as friends. Anyway he probably didn't even give her a real number to call, which had happened to Sarah before. She never did understand why guys did that, when she was younger she would be all excited and call only to find the number didn't exist or was for a doctor's surgery. Why did guys promise things they just didn't mean? If they didn't want to see her again they could have just said, she could have taken it.

'Sarah, so what do you think?'

Alice's voice brought her back to the present.

'I think it is lovely, a really nice office. I love the Nespresso machine, brilliant gadget. Show me the planning tools and I will get down to work.' She was raring to go.

'Sarah, can you call our aristocrat and arrange a meeting with him. In the meantime, I suggest you come up with a few potential ideas for the party of the year and research various alternative options and likely prices. We need to show him we are really thorough and have sought out only the best and most unusual ideas for his event. Like I said before, he is really fussy.'

Sarah dialled the number, she had dealt with some difficult people in the past she was certain she could handle anything that this work would throw at her.

A man answered 'Fawsett House, Thomas Fawsett speaking.'

'Oh good morning Thomas, My name is Sarah and I am calling from 'Perfect Events' I am handling the party for you and wondered if we could meet to chat in more detail about your requirements.'

'Sarah, Good to hear from you, that sounds fabulous, it would be great to meet and discuss. Thursday is good for me, let's not make it so formal, how does a Jazz evening at Pizza Express sound?'

Sarah had enjoyed the Jazz evening, perhaps a little too much if the next day was anything to go by. This was however, going to be a business meeting. She wanted to suggest a daytime meeting but Alice had made it clear that this was an important client, so what he requested went. The customer was always right after all.

'Thursday, Pizza Express is good for me Thomas, see you then.'

'See you then Sarah, oh you can call me Tommy by the way.'

Sarah ended the call and put the appointment in the diary. Pizza Express twice in one week, she hoped the waitress wouldn't recognize her.

'Thomas sounded nice Alice, he has a gorgeous posh accent, oh and he has already said I can call him Tommy.'

'That sounds promising,' Alice agreed.

Sarah was kept busy all morning researching ideas, this new job was so much fun. Sure she used to chat to David and write the odd letter and although she had enjoyed it at the time, it turns out there was more out there for her to discover and even more to conquer in her life.

At lunchtime Sarah and Alice headed to All Bar One for a glass of wine and a bite to eat. Alice knew the bar staff well as she had held many client meetings in there. Lunchtimes were jam packed but the staff had helpfully reserved a table for them. Sarah looked around, so many suits. Oh a man in a suit, her heart felt pained she missed David and then there he was standing right beside her. Adam!

'Hey Sarah, we meet again.'

'Adam!' She felt herself blushing.

His suit was sharp and tailored, showing off the gym toned arms and the shirt crisp white made the whites of his eyes whiter. She gazed into his stunning blue eyes and wondered why she hadn't called him yet.

'Sarah, you never called.'

'I am sorry, I have had a few things on my mind of late AND I have been quite busy, besides surely it hasn't been THAT long has it?'

'Feels like an eternity, but you know what? Us meeting again like this has to mean something, it was obviously fate that we met at all.'

Sarah's legs felt like jelly, she was wobbling all over the place. Thank goodness she was sat down. How did he manage to have such an effect on her?

Alice came back from ordering from the bar and just like Sarah had done did a double take at the handsome stranger before them. Sarah noticed she too was transfixed by his hypnotic blue eyes.

'Hi, I am Alice. I don't believe Sarah has mentioned you before.'

'Adam'. He put his arm out to shake her hand. 'I would join you but I have to get back to the office, Sarah call me!'

'Who was that?'

'Adam.'

'Yes I know that is Adam but who is he, I want details.'

'Oh there's nothing to tell, we met in Starbucks the other day. He gave me his number and I haven't called, end of story.'

'Why ever not?'

'In case you have forgotten Alice I already have a boyfriend.'

'And he already has a wife, there is nothing stopping you.'

'Maybe I will, I just need a bit of time to think.'

'Give me his number, I will call him,' Alice said sounding a little too eager.

'Can we get back to the Office?' Sarah felt a little unsettled and had lost her appetite.

'Go ahead if you want, I have planned to meet a few friends for drinks, Sarah you haven't eaten anything yet.'

Sarah's stomach rumbled, perhaps she should stay for a bite to eat. Soon the wine and chat was flowing and she had forgotten all about the handsome stranger.

Sarah's phone beeped, a text from David.

'How about a weekend away? Your suggestion. I miss you x'

Sarah thought about it for a few seconds before sending a reply.

'Miss you too, Nice sounds nice x'

She knew she was being cheeky but he owed her.

'Consider it done, I will be over Friday night, see you then x'

CHAPTER FOUR

The days whizzed by and soon it was Thursday. Sarah still hadn't texted Adam, after their chance encounter in All Bar One it was obvious he was still interested and surely it wouldn't harm to make him wait a little longer. But then again exactly how long would he be prepared to wait before losing interest?

Still she convinced herself, life was good right now, why upset the apple cart.

Sarah called Tommy to confirm things were still ok for their meeting later that evening.

'Sarah! Good to hear from you. No, all ok at this end. Looking forward to it.'

Alice had been out of the office for the last two days so

Sarah had just taken some sandwiches in and eaten them at her desk. Lunchtimes were spent surfing the net and planning things to do in Nice although as it was just a weekend there wasn't going to be much time to do very much at all.

Alice called 'Good luck Sarah.'

'Thanks Alice, don't you worry about a thing I have it all under control.'

'OK, I shall be back in the office tomorrow, let's have a meeting at 10am and you can update me then.'

'OK night.'

Sarah packed up for the evening and brought out her makeup bag. A quick spruce up at her desk and she would be ready to go. She applied powder to remove the shine from her face and had a quick spray of Batiste Dry Shampoo in the hair for some extra va va voom. With her lipstick doubling up as a blusher she now had a cute looking natural flush on her cheeks and coordinating gorgeously pouty lips. The last thing she did was spritz her perfume all over and headed out into the night.

Walking into Pizza Express she hoped she had arrived first, it wasn't done to arrive after the client. Not professional at all. Of course she had no idea what he looked like, she had managed to resist the temptation to google his name or picture.

Oh wonderful! The same waitress as before. A glint of recognition showed in her eyes but it didn't matter Sarah thought, this was not a date this was a business meeting and so what if I am here again I like Pizza.

'

'Table for two madam?' The waitress was pleasant.

'Erm yes please.'

As she sat down concealed behind a huge plant pot she wondered how they would recognise each other when he did arrive. Of course! She had a brainwave – Look out for the man in a cravat, all aristocrats wear them.

And then he appeared through the door looking like he had been dragged through a bush. He was not what Sarah had been expecting at all. Mind you she had never met an aristocrat before, her only view of them was from films or from photographs on the Society pages of the magazines she liked to read who regularly featured fancy Society Parties.

He made a quick sweep of the room and noticed these eyes focussed on him, it must be Sarah. Walking over to her he spotted a mirror and took in his appearance. Messy, it would have to do.

'Sarah? Tommy.'

'Hello there, I see you found it ok.'

Tommy liked the look of Sarah, her smile was sweet and innocent he thought. She looked terribly professional except for this smear of lipstick across her face, I wonder if she knows…He smiled to himself. Yes, he thought, we are going to get on.

'So have you been here before Sarah? I have never been although I hear the Jazz is good.'

'Oh yes, well once before. It's nice and the chocolate cake is to die for.'

'I should think we shall start with a bottle of wine and go from there, well obviously we will order from the menu!'

Sarah laughed, relaxing immediately. She had a feeling this was going to be a good evening. Tommy seemed so nice for someone so rich.

The waitress appeared ready to take their order and Sarah could have sworn she saw her eyebrow raise when they ordered a bottle of wine. It was almost as if she had remembered how Sarah had walked out of there the last time she had visited. Of course she could have just been imagining it.

'So I have been looking at a few options and I can tell you I am very excited about this party. Such a fabulous idea!' 'One thing I forgot to ask, is there any particular reason for it?'

'Hmmm? Oh yes! It is a sort of thank goodness that relationship is over party.'

'Really? That is hilarious!'

'Is it? I am serious. I am so grateful it is over, my girlfriend was ahem a little crazy. I want to thank all my friends for being there and this is going to be the night for a new start.'

'Well, I suppose it takes all reasons. I am sorry I laughed.'

'No worries. It is cool. Like I said that chapter of my life is OVER.'

'Well, so I was thinking actors in costumes, serving staff in costume. Fireworks, props, themed rooms, spooky music and that is just the start.'

'Mmm, yeah! Sounds good!'

'Do you want more details tonight or are you happy for me to send it over to you?'

'Whatever you wish. I thought tonight I could get to know the lady handling the event, get to know you better, what makes you tick.'

'I could show you a few of the parties we have done before so you can get an idea of what Perfect Events is about if you like?'

'Oh I know what you do Sarah. But who is the girl behind the company?'

'Oh that is Alice, I am her assistant now.'

'Yes I have met Alice, she is an incredibly driven lady. So tell me about you.'

The dough balls arrived and they were working their way through them when she noticed melted garlic butter dribbling down his chin. He had what looked like a few days growth and a strand of parsley was just sat there. She couldn't help but stare.

'Me, not much to say really. This is new venture for me but my background has always been in organisation and planning. Alice is my best friend and I guess right now all the jigsaw pieces are falling into place.'

'You dating?'

Sarah wasn't sure what this had to do with work but found herself saying 'No, not right now,' which if she thought about it was technically true.

'Fantastic, so you will be ploughing all your energy into planning my event,' he winked at her.

'In the words of an X Factor judge, 110%'

'Enough business talk, let's listen to the Jazz, it seems a waste to come here and not.'

Sarah put away her file and tucked into her pizza. The Jazz music being played made her stop in her tracks.

'It Had To Be You!' She recognised it from When Harry Met Sally. Right now it was when Tommy met Sarah.

He was smiling at her, she noticed he had been doing it a lot this evening. It felt like they were caught up in the moment. They both mouthed 'I Love This Film.'

She could feel her cheeks burning, focus Sarah this is a business meeting and he is the client. Stay professional. Besides, if anything DID happen he was so obviously on the rebound. Never a good time to get involved.

Beneath those curtains, his eyes peered through. He had such friendly eyes that smiled even when his mouth wasn't. Oh and there goes that smile again, this time showing his perfect set of teeth.

Alice hadn't mentioned he was cute in a foppish kind of way. She could have warned me Sarah thought. Sarah wondered what was wrong with her, she wasn't in the habit of falling for every guy she met although right now it certainly felt like it.

Wrongity, wrong she reminded herself.

'Sorry, what?'

Oh there she had only gone and done it again, said it out loud.

'Nothing! Coffee?'

'Well clearly you are insisting, why not go the whole hog and have dessert as well!'

They both ordered a latte and the famous Pizza Express chocolate fudge cake and devouring it in seconds indicated to each other that both had crumbs left on the face. He couldn't resist leaning over and helping Sarah with hers and she felt something inside her tingle.

This time she was too full of food to feel tipsy and managed to walk out of the restaurant in a straight line.

'Well, goodnight Sarah, no doubt I will be speaking to you tomorrow, it has been fun.'

'Goodbye Tommy,' she wished he had insisted that she call him Thomas. Tommy was so informal he felt like a friend already, one she was going to get along very nicely with.

The theme tune of Taxi was playing inside and that reminded her to hail one home.

CHAPTER FIVE

Sarah submitted her expenses claim and Alice looked down at it.

'How was he? Looks like you had a good night.'

'Yes I am sorry, I wasn't sure how much we could have on expenses, is this ok?'

'Of course, he is our biggest client to date. You have to spend to accumulate.'

'You never mentioned what he looked like, you never said he was attractive.'

'Is he? I didn't notice, I hope you behaved yourself

young lady,' she teased her.

'Yes I did, best behaviour!'

'So, are you ready for our update meeting?'

'Sure am, I will grab us some coffees.'

An hour later and the meeting had finished.

'Well, I have to say Sarah I am impressed. You have been so thorough in your research and those calculations are so specific. I am liking your ideas a lot. You could run through the same with Tommy or narrow it down giving him a few choices. How you handle it is entirely up to you. Once decisions are made, set up meetings with the suppliers. Good work.'

Sarah felt pleased, it was so nice to get feedback for the job she was doing. The rest of the afternoon was spent creating spreadsheets and a PowerPoint presentation complete with appropriately themed music. Event planning, yes she had found her niche.

Her phone beeped – Text from David.

'Hey Sweets, all set for our naughty little weekend away?'

'Davey boy' Did she really type that? 'It could not come soon enough'

Soon they were on their way, David had bought her a little perfume gift from Duty Free. She guessed he wanted her to wear it whilst they were on their trip.

They kissed and held hands just like a normal couple, why couldn't she have him for ever? Why did he have to go back to his wife? Yes, she knew it was because of the kids but they would surely be happier in a house that didn't have arguments. David had told her that not a day went by when he and Laura didn't argue about one thing or another. This also made Sarah wonder why Laura stayed with David. Surely she would be much better off with someone else if their life was such a misery. It had to be the money and lifestyle that David brought home. Sarah would never stay with someone just for the lifestyle, she had to be happy in all aspects of her relationship she decided. Except here she was with a guy who just couldn't or was it he wouldn't commit to her.

Sarah found herself drifting off, this week had been utterly exhausting. Having coasted in her job for a few years she had actually had to do some real work and whilst it had been fun it had also been physically and mentally taking its toll. Commuting, meetings and research. She liked being busy though and wouldn't change it for the world.

'Darling, we are here.'

'Sorry, I must have dozed off.'

'Not to worry, we all need a power nap now and then, besides you look adorable when you are asleep, my little angel.'

It may have been meant in an endearing way but she found herself muttering 'Patronizing, much.'

David didn't hear however, he was busy getting their weekend bags out of the overhead cabins almost knocking off the head of the passenger still sat down in front of them.

He really didn't care about others Sarah thought. Why was she thinking negative thoughts, before she had only ever seen the good in David? In her eyes he could do no wrong and yet it felt like something had changed. Almost overnight, he was beginning to irritate her.

She was finding him overbearing and brash. The gifts were nice but it felt like he was trying to buy her silence, trying to keep her sweet so she wouldn't tell the wife. She resolved to enjoy herself, it was Nice after all but she would see how she felt at the end of this weekend. She wanted to issue an ultimatum to him – The wife or her. Was she brave enough to raise the issue, she wasn't sure. Then again, it wasn't like she was lacking potential suitors, she still hadn't texted Adam. Was he the fall back option? Hardly, the guy was like a god. If she had to think of a chocolate to describe him she would have said a dreamy Cadbury's Flake…Swoon.

At the hotel, the reception that greeted them was a stunning lesson in architecture with all white marble flooring and stunning white columns, A gold and glass domed ceiling contained the biggest and most imposing crystal chandelier to be found in France. The bedroom was a huge romantic lair of elegance and refinement. Rose petals were laid out on the bed upping the romantic levels. A Champagne bottle was sat in an ice bucket chilling on the bedside table. In the bathroom she found a welcoming Jacuzzi bath. David however was engrossed in checking his phone and emails. Sarah turned on the bath, undressed, laid back and relaxed in the warm bubbles.

Next morning she woke up to find both her and David's faces covered in what looked like smeared mud. What on earth had they got up to last night? She tried hard to remember but just couldn't. Had she really drunk too much again? She removed the mud from her face and took it to her nose to sniff. Not mud, chocolate. Oh and there were the wrappers! The hotel had left some chocolate on their pillows. They hadn't seen them and fallen asleep on them.

'Oh ha ha' she laughed to herself. David was still fast asleep. She got up and dressed. Breakfast would be served shortly and she was feeling hungry.

Coffee, croissants and fruit. Oh this place was like heaven to her, the white marble surroundings resembling billowing clouds and she adored the beautiful green and gold period furniture. The day passed quickly as they headed into Nice on the bus and spent the day just relaxing with each other on the pebbly beach and taking in, albeit briefly, the sights that Nice possessed. Food was quite simply a gastronomical treat as they dined in the best seafront restaurants - for lunch they enjoyed delicious Moules et Frites. At dinner Sarah was treated to the delights of a Michelin Starred restaurant and indulged in a three course meal of seared scallops to start, an exquisite and fleshy Cod with greens for main and a rich and intense chocolate tarte for dessert. She was having the time of her life, what an incredible way to spend a weekend, although she knew that all good things had to come to end. All too soon it was time to head to the airport and fly home.

CHAPTER SIX

Monday morning brought Sarah bumping right down back to earth. The Northern Line wasn't running, it was pouring with rain and the buses were passing by her completely full and refusing to stop. How could life be so changeable? She wished she was back in wonderful and nice Nice.

She got her phone out to tell Alice that she was going to be late when she accidently dialled Adam's number instead. She tried to stop the call but he had picked up immediately. She was forced to speak.

'Now I am going to put all my money on this being the forlorn girl I met in Starbucks,' she heard Adam say.

'Are you talking to me?' She replied.

'I knew it! How the devil are you Sarah and to what do I owe this pleasure?'

'Actually I meant to call Alice.'

'Oh,' she imagined his head falling down sad again.

'It seems though my phone had other ideas. You kept talking about fate when we met, maybe this is what you meant?'

'I was hoping you would call, I would love to take you to dinner if you would allow me?'

'Oh what the hell, go on then!'

'Don't sound too eager now Sarah.'

'Sorry, I am having a hell of a morning. I was supposed to be in work twenty minutes ago and I am nowhere near. I would have walked but these stupid heels are not exactly suitable for the puddle ridden journey.'

'So….what else are you wearing? I am trying to conjure up an image here.'

'Shut up!'

'It was a joke. Anyway I best get back to work. Pizza Express tomorrow night?'

'Can we make it Thursday?' She didn't want to come across too keen.

'Good plan, I hear they have a fabulous Jazz evening.'

Oh great, what was it with men and Jazz Evenings and this bizarre obsession with Pizza Express. As far as first dates go it wasn't a bad place to go to but this was getting to be a bit of a habit. Three times in less than two weeks was more than a little careless. She really hoped the waitress with the raised eyebrow was owed a day off!

Once in the office she helped herself to an espresso and settled down to work. Alice walked over to her desk.

'Good weekend?'

'The best thanks.'

'I don't know how you do it Sarah. Your life is a rollercoaster. Ditch David and find someone nice. Someone who is available for you all the time. I promised myself I wouldn't say anything but I just can't see you getting hurt. I won't let it happen to you. You are too nice for him. Sure he is spoiling you at the moment but it isn't a real relationship, can't you see that?'

'Alice please, I know what I am doing,' Sarah was annoyed. Alice was a fine one to talk. All through University she had been having an affair with her married tutor. Then it had been Sarah begging her to leave him, saying things would only result in heartbreak. Two terms in Alice had walked into the lecture hall to meet him to find him in a passionate embrace with another student. She ran out crying. He hadn't followed. Heartbroken she asked to switch tutors and decided to concentrate on her studies, declaring herself off of men for life, claiming all men were idiots and cheats who couldn't be trusted.

Since then she had had one serious relationship with a nice but boring guy (In Sarah's opinion) but that had fizzled out after a couple of years. Sometimes people just fall out of love she had told Sarah. No reason for it, it just happened. Alice spent all her time on her business and the rest socialising with friends. Relationships could wait as far as she was concerned.

'Alice, are you jealous?'

'Of what exactly? You? Your relationship with a married

man? You of all people should know how it all ends. If he does it with you, he will do it with others. Trust me.'

'David's different,' Sarah muttered under her breath.

'And if you think David's different you will soon realise he is just like the rest. You mark my words.'

Just then her phone beeped – Tommy.

'Hey gorgeous, how is that planning coming along? I think we need another meeting. An art gallery?'

Sarah was pretty sure this sounded more like a date. Or perhaps he meant to have the meeting in the canteen. That was the thing with an Events Company, they could hold meetings just about anywhere. Relaxed and informal that is how they liked to do business.

'Tomorrow is great, I have a few updates for you actually.'

'Look forward to it.'

'Alice I am going to be out of the office in the afternoon. Meeting Tommy.'

'Fine,' replied Alice rather tersely.

Sarah was doubting herself, maybe working with your best friend wasn't such a good idea after all. Sarah wanted to prove to her friend that she could plan the party of the century and she was going to do it with or without her help.

CHAPTER SEVEN

Tommy and Sarah met on the steps of the National Gallery, thank god the pigeons had now been removed from Trafalgar Square she thought. As a child Sarah's family had liked nothing better than to spend a lazy afternoon there and she was fascinated with the bird people who would be covered from top to toe in pigeons. She would stand and stare at them while her sister would climb up to the Lions to sit on them and get a better view from up high. She would shout and wave to her parent's below whilst hoping no one else would come to knock her off. Sarah loved those happy days and used to be excited when her parents would suggest to go there. Until the day her parents bought her a bag of seeds to feed the birds and she suddenly found her herself surrounded by pecking vermin and then one pooped on her shoulder. Her parents shooed the pigeons away and tried to placate their crying daughter. But to no avail, she was inconsolable and from that day on had such a dislike of pigeons and Trafalgar Square that the family had to make other plans of how to spend their Sundays.

Sarah eyed a sole pigeon and started running up the steps to avoid its gaze. Flapping her arms around and yelping Tommy couldn't help but look on in bemusement, realizing she was running into the building he ran after her.

'Sarah, wait up.'

He found Sarah inside taking deep breaths.

'Are you ok? What just happened out there?'

'Pigeons,' she panted. 'I can't stand them.'

He burst into laughter 'Are you serious?' He noticed she wasn't laughing. 'That is quite a problem in London. They are everywhere!'

'Tell me about it!'

Sarah prepared her bag to be searched and they went inside.

She had never been to the National Gallery. The ceilings were high and the rooms were vast. All around her people were standing and staring at the paintings. Every so often there were benches to sit on. A nice place to come and contemplate she thought.

Tommy had walked on ahead, he turned round revealing a mischievous grin.

'You are gorgeous, you know that,' he said.

Sarah blushed, 'Tommy please! Can we get down to business?'

'Ooh you are forward!' Tommy couldn't believe his luck. Perhaps his charms were melting her heart already.

'You know very well what I mean!' They sat on her bench and she got out her Ipad and started the presentation. Complete with fancy images and a demo run through of the evening and its timings.

'I love it!' He declared.

'To be honest Sarah I trust you to know what you are doing, I gave you the budget and I am happy to listen to you and give you full control of the party.'

'But, I would like some input. This isn't a surprise party for a five year old. This has the potential to be the party of the year.' She instantly regretted saying it but it was too late the words were already out of her mouth.

Comparing her client to a five year had been such a bad idea.

Tommy started laughing hysterically. 'You don't know me, maybe a five year old's party is just what I had in mind! My parents do keep telling me to grow up!'

'Seriously though – I am looking for a Count Dracula themed party in a castle. All the little details I am happy to leave with you. Oh and I will need a costume, I am going to be Count Dracula of course! Lots of red wine flowing and gory inspired food. We eat anything.'

'One last request – you simply have to be there. Can you dress up too?' He was hopeful.

'Well of course I will attend. Just to make sure that everything runs to plan you understand. And no to any costumes. I have my professional integrity to keep intact.'

Tommy's bottom lip came out. He looked very sad, like Sarah had just broken his heart.

'Pretty please, you can be my damsel in distress?'

It was Sarah's turn to laugh 'I probably WILL be a damsel in distress if the party isn't going well!'

'I will see what I can do, NO promises.'

Sarah was pretty sure Alice would prefer they remained in black business attire throughout the evening. But then again Tommy was pretty unconventional, this wasn't just any old party and Alice had said 'What the client wants, the client gets…'

The rest of their planned meeting was spent wandering around the gallery, it was a beautiful and peaceful afternoon, and she felt she could stay there forever locked away from the real world and all its trials and tribulations. She ignored her phone buzzing manically in her bag. It could wait. After all if she had been in a real meeting she wouldn't be answering her phone.

Tommy tried to hold her hand when they were looking at a particularly romantic painting but she eased hers away and folded her arms, all the while looking avidly at the painting as if she was deep in thought and he soon got the message and gave up on the idea.

They ended their day together with a coffee. He ordered a cappuccino and didn't say no to some chocolate powder sprinkled on the top. She opted for a latte. She noticed him once again gazing at her.

'What are you doing?'

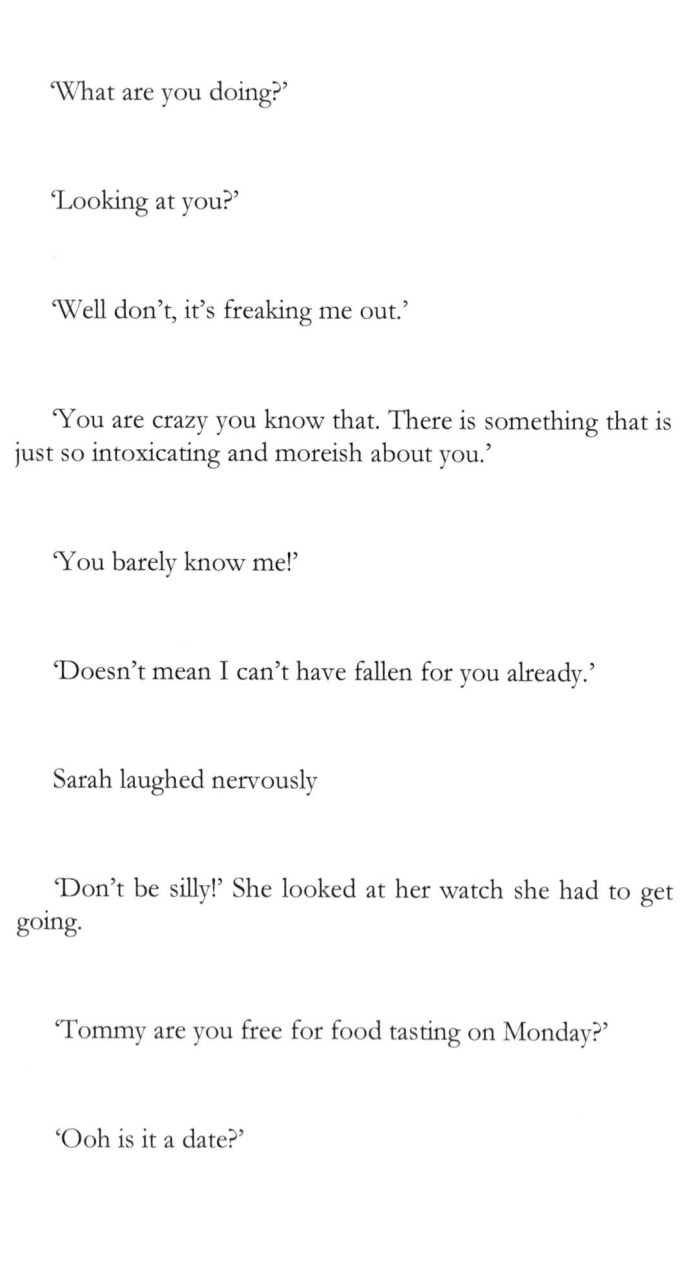

'Looking at you?'

'Well don't, it's freaking me out.'

'You are crazy you know that. There is something that is just so intoxicating and moreish about you.'

'You barely know me!'

'Doesn't mean I can't have fallen for you already.'

Sarah laughed nervously

'Don't be silly!' She looked at her watch she had to get going.

'Tommy are you free for food tasting on Monday?'

'Ooh is it a date?'

Inside she felt all warm and gooey. She really liked Tommy and his naughty school boy behaviour. Outwardly however she gave no clues. Ignoring his question she remained business-like.

'Meet me on Monday at Old Street Station at 9.30am. We shall be going on a culinary journey.'

'I must dash,' she cried out 'date with my hairdresser,' and as fast as he could open his mouth she had disappeared.

Once outside she finally glanced at her phone.

Five missed phone calls, two voicemails and one text message from Alice, three messages from David and one from Adam.

She worked her way through them.

Adam – 'Hey, can't wait for our date x'

David – 'Missing you x' 'Do you miss me too?' 'Are you ok?'

Alice – 'Hey, It's Alice, I just wanted to say I am sorry'

'Hey, I know you are busy with Tommy today but call me after and let me know how it went'.

'Love you x'.

Sarah felt guilty. Perhaps she should have answered her phone. Her stomach lurched when she saw the message from Adam. He seemed keen but still she couldn't help wondering why he liked her so much. She was starting to tire of David, he was coming across as desperate and a little needy. He was not the man she had met or fallen in love with. Alice had sounded genuinely sorry, she felt bad. She should call her and clear the air. Sarah and Alice had always had each other to rely on and to fall out over a man was just plain stupid. They were too old for this carry on.

She dialled Sarah's number. No answer. It went to answerphone.

'Hey, it's just me. Love you too. Just to let you know everything is going well with the party planning and Tommy seems happy to leave it to me. Seems his reputation is not in tune with how I am finding him. He seems pretty relaxed and not difficult at all. Anyway I guess I will see you tomorrow. Bye.'

CHAPTER EIGHT

Sarah ran through the food menu and made appointments to meet the suppliers for Monday. Everything was shaping up nicely and she started to relax as the afternoon wore on. Alice was out of the office again and bar a few enquiry phone calls which Sarah had taken it was pretty quiet.

Alice hadn't called back yet so she guessed she was snowed under with work and client meetings. Sarah was happy to let her contact her when she was ready. She wouldn't chase. Her mind wandered to affairs of the heart.

Butterflies raced in Sarah's stomach. Tonight was the night of her date with Adam. The day had finally arrived and now Sarah was having second thoughts. Should she call him and cancel. She had an idea, she would send him a message as that would be easier and that way she wouldn't have to actually speak to him.

Fate. There was that word again. Perhaps she should let fate deal with this. She would go, it wouldn't harm her to go on just one date. Who knows, perhaps he would turn out to be an utter bore. All good looks and no substance. Although she had bumped into him twice now she still knew nothing about him except his name. Yes, she decided she would go, it may be a laugh or it might be a mistake but at least she would know once and for all. If it all went pear shaped she would just delete his number from her phone and forget she had ever met him.

This time she left work early and went home to get ready. She had a quick shower to freshen up. A pair of skinny black jeans, white shirt and statement necklace later, she looked in the mirror. She liked this look a lot. It didn't look like she had gone to TOO much effort but was elegant and with no skin on show, respectable. She completed her look with smoky eyes and nude lip-gloss. Make up done and a spritz of Chanel and she was ready for her date.

She noticed that each time she hit a zebra crossing the cars would stop to let her pass. One guy yelled out 'Oi, Oi' Part of her wanted to be annoyed but another part of her was pleased that she was getting a reaction like this. Adam was so damn handsome she wanted to look the part when she saw him and feel gorgeous too. The beautiful couple, that's what they would be.

As she entered Pizza Express she noticed him sat down already. His piercing blue eyes were focused on the door and she felt his eyes looking her up and down. She could feel her cheeks getting hotter and hoped she hadn't gone too red.

'Sarah! I am so glad you came. You look fabulous and smell wonderful,' she was sure she felt his lips brush her neck but she couldn't be a hundred per cent certain.

'Thanks Adam, You don't look too bad yourself!'

It was true he looked stunning in his grey suit and white shirt. She had a real soft spot for a man in a suit and when he looked as good as Adam did in it well it would be criminal not to show it off. Oh and you smell so good she thought. Warm and spicy. Manly, so manly. She felt faint.

Sarah looked around, there was no sign of the waitress with the raised eyebrow. Phew. Unfortunately for Sarah it wasn't the waitress's day off and she soon appeared from wherever she had been hiding.

She walked over to Sarah and Adam and handed them the menu. As she handed Sarah's to her Sarah was sure she gave her a look of disdain and raised the other eyebrow as she said 'Madam' a little too ferociously.

'Bottle of white wine for Madam?'

Sarah felt all flustered, she must remember to email

Pizza Express tomorrow to complain about the waitress who had absolutely no idea how to behave discreetly. Quite frankly it was none of her business who Sarah ate with.

Pulling herself together she replied, confidently.

'None for me thank you, I don't drink. I shall have a coke please.'

The waitress snorted.

Adam ordered a Peroni Beer and during this bemusing exchange had already decided on the pizza he was going to have and ordered that as well. Sarah ordered a lighter pizza with the salad in the centre.

'What was that all about?'

'I have no idea,' breezed Sarah. She wasn't about to say she had already been here twice before each time with a different man and the waitress was clearly disapproving or jealous, Sarah wasn't entirely sure which.

The waitress brought their drinks and placed Sarah's in front of her muttering under her breath 'Humph no drink.'

Sarah ignored her, she could wait. She would send her revenge email tomorrow, the waitress would get the sack and Sarah could return here to her heart's content.

'So did you come straight from work?'

'Yes, I did. For some reason today was a really busy one.'

'What is it that you do?'

'Oh I don't want to bore you, just stuff.'

'Adam, I know absolutely nothing about you. I am sure you do more than just 'stuff.'

'There is plenty of time for all that.'

'You seem pretty confident.'

That was the problem with the good looking guys, they were used to women falling at their feet that they didn't seem to want or need to make an effort. Sarah wasn't going to make it easy for him.

'There might not be another time, suppose I don't want

to see you again?'

'Well then I guess you will never know…'

Well that ultimatum didn't work.

'So tell me sad girl, what was making you sad that day in Starbucks?'

'Oh I don't want to bore you,' two can play that game Sarah thought.

'Touché,' Adam chuckled.

'Anyway I am not sad anymore and I don't want to look back. Onwards and upwards as they say.'

'So what made you decide that you would go on a date with me, I take it you are single?'

Sarah thought, this was a first date. She wasn't committing to a lifetime with him, He didn't need to know about David and at the moment Tommy and her were just good friends.

'I am, no harm in seeing what is around is there?'

'No harm at all,' he agreed.

They spent the evening flirting with each other, they questioned each other on what made their ideal partner. He jokingly described her and she describing him in return. They talked about their likes and dislikes. Finding that they had plenty in common made Sarah feel that she had been right to agree to a date with him. It was nice to be out with someone who didn't seem to have any motive than just simply being on a date.

They even committed the cardinal sin of discussing past relationships. She found him opening up, being honest and sincere and even sharing his fears for the future with her. It seemed like they both wanted the same thing – to love and to be loved.

Sarah realised that they had been so engrossed in each other that suddenly she became aware that now the restaurant had emptied right out and the last song was being announced. A rendition of Norah Jones 'If You Want The Rainbow, You Must Have The Rain' Such a beautiful song and full of truthful lyrics. It must be time for her rainbow. She had seen enough of the rain.

She smiled and then she noticed in the corner of her eye that pesky waitress pointing at the clock and gesturing with her arms for Sarah to leave. How flipping rude she thought.

Luckily Adam hadn't noticed, he seemed to be deep in thought. Somewhere far away. The power of Norah, romance was most definitely in the air.

Outside the spell was broken. The warmth they had felt cut cruelly by the biting, icy wind. She wanted to get home and bounced from foot to foot, rubbing her hands together.

'You are cold. Let me see you home.'

She let him lead the way until he stopped and said 'Where is home by the way?'

Sarah contemplated offering him in for a nightcap but thought better of it. It had been a wonderful, romantic evening. The last thing she wanted to do was ruin it by doing something stupid so soon. If he was keen to take it further he would wait. She put the key in the front door and turned around.

'Well thanks for a lovely evening Adam.'

'I have enjoyed myself too, I would love to see you again.'

Sarah flashed a smile at him. Wearing her heart on her sleeve she whispered.

'Me too.'

'I will call you.'

'I'll be waiting.'

She closed the door behind her. She found him irresistible and had she left the door open a moment longer he would have probably have found himself inside her flat with her. She could feel herself literally glowing with happiness.

The date had been amazing. Conversation had flowed and of course he was incredibly easy on the eye.

She hadn't felt like this about any man in such a long time. Was this it. Had she found the one?

Her phone beeped. A text from David.

'Hope you are in tomorrow morning. David x'

CHAPTER NINE

Next morning she awoke to the noise of the doorbell being rung. She opened the door to find a man holding the largest bouquet of flowers she had ever seen.

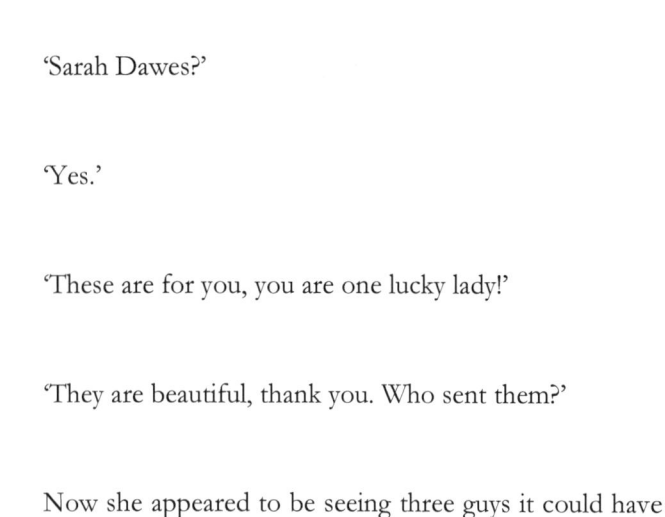

'Sarah Dawes?'

'Yes.'

'These are for you, you are one lucky lady!'

'They are beautiful, thank you. Who sent them?'

Now she appeared to be seeing three guys it could have potentially come from any one of them.

'There's card. Have a nice day.'

Sarah found the card and opened it up.

'Sarah my darling. I am so sorry I haven't given you much attention recently. I hope this delivery goes some way to showing you how much I care. I will make it up to you I promise. David x'

She texted David.

'Thanks for the flowers, they are stunning. I am a bit busy in the next few days but next week would be good for meeting up'

The flowers were lovely but nothing made up for the lack of attention he was giving her. Oddly she had barely given David a second thought with everything else that was going on in her life. Perhaps the relationship was coming to its natural end. She didn't end the text with a kiss.

She made herself a strong coffee and heard her phone beeping again. A text from Adam.

'Can't stop thinking about you'

She smiled. What a nice text to receive. So she guessed Adam wasn't going to be a one hit wonder after all. She wouldn't reply straightaway, not wanting to appear over eager.

She showered and then checked her phone again. Nothing from Alice. She called Alice and it went to answerphone.

'Hey, guess you are on the tube right now. Speak to you when I get in.'

Alice was already at her desk when Sarah arrived.

'I got your messages, sorry I haven't replied. Been snowed under. I have three event all happening at the same time and to be honest I am having to be in multiple places at once. I am SO tired. I just want to say I AM sorry, and you are right I have no right to be interfering. I won't say another word.'

'Alice, I went on a date with Adam,' Sarah blurted out.

'You saucy minx! And you never said a word! Well, what was he like?'

'Really, really nice. It was just incredible. It has been so long since I went on a date like that, I barely slept all night I was just lying awake thinking of him.'

'Does he know about David?'

'No, it was just a first date. It didn't seem necessary to tell him. How was I supposed to know it was going to go so well? Besides, I don't think there is going to be a David much longer. I don't seem to feel the same way about him any more.'

'Tell him it's over, sooner rather than later. Otherwise things could get messy all round.'

'I know, I will,' Sarah promised.

'Alice, can I help you with any of these projects? The party of the century has pretty much stalled until we go on a tasting spree on Monday.'

Alice was grateful for the offer and soon the two of them were busy sharing ideas and workload. Heads down they made great headway with all the outstanding tasks. Their friendship happily back on track, equilibrium restored once more.

Sarah's concentration was disrupted by the sound of a

text coming through on her phone.

It was her mother.

'Sarah dear, can you possibly make a trip up to see us this weekend. I don't like to ask but it's your dad. He's not been well.'

She felt sick. She dialled her mum immediately.

'Mum, it's me. What is the matter, is dad OK? Of course I will come right away.'

'Oh my darling. He is in hospital having tests. We just don't know what is wrong. He collapsed at home when I was out shopping,' Sarah's mum could barely get the words out through her tears.

Alice said she could leave right away and Sarah took the train up to Oxford where she was met by her sister Charlotte.

Charlotte had been crying, her eyes were all bloodshot and puffy. Sarah gave her a big hug and they just held each other close for a while.

'Oh Sarah. What if he isn't going to be ok?'

'He will be,' Sarah reassured Charlotte. As the older sister her role had always been to be the sensible one. The dependable one that they could rely on to hold the fort and lend support. Sarah hadn't minded she quite enjoyed being the older sister. Right now however whilst she wanted to break down and have a good cry herself she felt she couldn't, not in front of Charlotte. She didn't want to panic her.

Sarah dropped her bag into her old room and collapsed onto her bed. Her room had remained unchanged since the day she had left. She loved her mum for that. Her parents had always said to her if she ever needed to come home, her room would always be there for her. Bambi was lying happily between her pillows. She picked up her childhood comforter and sobbed into its fur.

'Dad please be ok,' she whispered.

Charlotte knocked on the door. 'Mum says come down for a bite to eat and then we will head to the hospital.'

Her mother apologised for serving beans on toast for dinner but said she had no life in her to do any more. Charlotte and Sarah reassured her it was fine. Neither felt that hungry but were grateful for the comfort food. Sarah asked her mum not to worry and promised her mum that she would cook for them whilst she was there.

On the way to the hospital Sarah's stomach was in knots. She felt sick with worry for her dad. He had been the joker of the family. He used to say silly jokes and make them all laugh or act like a clown. During the day he had worked at the council in a responsible job for the Health and Safety department, but whenever the girls would ask what he did he used to tell them that he could tell them but he would have to kill them afterwards. 'Top secret important work' he would say and tap his nose.

Her dad had retired last year after working 40 years for the council and spent his days in his allotment and seeing his friends. The Dawes were still very much in love and both Charlotte and Sarah held them up as their example of a perfect marriage. If they could find a partner as perfect as dad and emulate their parents success then lifelong happiness would surely follow.

But modern life was different. People travelled further. They were encouraged to be more ambitious, and to have their own hobbies and interests and a separate life outside the home. In Sarah's mother's day it was pretty much unheard of for them to have girlie weekends or night's out and now it was seen as pretty much essential.

Sarah wished she had a crystal ball to know what life had in store for her. She would take a peek just once. That is all. Would she have a happy ever after or would she be one of those whose sad story was played out on Jeremy Kyle for all to ogle at.

They all marched through the hospital until they reached her dad's bed. He was lying there unresponsive. He must be sleeping. Although she didn't know how anyone would be able to sleep with the rackets going on, there were tubes attached to him everywhere and machines bleeping loudly beside his bed. She felt a single tear drop down her face and quickly wiped it away with her sleeve. Compose yourself Sarah, your family need you to be strong she willed herself.

She took her dad's hand and held it in her own. It brought back memories of how he would hold her hand when she was a child. She remembered how he had always had strong, firm hands and that if he would hold her a little too tight she would complain that he was hurting her. He would laugh and say that he was sorry and that Superheroes didn't know their own strength. When she was five she had really thought that her dad was Superman.

Dad's hand was limp now and nothing like that big, strong man that she held so dearly in her memory. She stroked it and squeezed it and told him that everything was going to be ok. He had his family around him and there they would stay.

She drifted away in her thoughts until she felt a hand on her shoulder.

'Sarah, visiting time is over. We have to go.'

'I am staying, Dad needs us here.'

A stern voice from across the room spoke up.

'I am afraid that isn't possible. You can come again tomorrow. The patients need their rest.'

Reluctantly Sarah left with Charlotte and her mum. That night she couldn't sleep. Her childhood flashed before her eyes. Memories of her dad were vivid and she felt like his presence was in the room. She felt like he was watching over her. How different to the night before when she couldn't sleep through feelings of new love.

Over the weekend Sarah spent all the time she could by his side, only going when asked to leave by the staff. Sarah felt torn between staying up in Oxford and returning to her job for Monday morning. She felt like she needed help in making a decision, a sign from above. And it came on Sunday evening. Her dad stirred and pulled off his oxygen mask.

'Get this damn thing off me!'

'Dad! Oh thank god!!'

He was still feeling weak but he was able to talk.

'I am ok love, don't you worry about me.'

'I do dad. I always will.'

The nurses said that things seemed to have improved significantly and the fact that Sarah had spoken to him meant that she felt comfortable enough to leave him and return to London with a promise of regular updates from mum and Charlotte and a promise from her that she would drop everything and return right away if anything changed.

CHAPTER TEN

Monday morning and back in the business world Sarah waited for Tommy at Old Street Tube for their food tasting day. He was late and she was beginning to get anxious. She kept checking her watch for the time and although she had made sure she had factored in likely delays and transport issues she hadn't anticipated for his tardiness. She tried calling him, no answer. If they didn't leave in the next five minutes they wouldn't make their first appointment on time. She was beginning to panic, what was keeping him?

Just as she was about to give up and go on alone she heard him calling her name.

'Sarah, wait up!' He was out of breath. She was annoyed. Client or no client. She didn't have time for this.

'Where on earth have you been?'

'Sorry! I am so sorry. I overslept and my mother didn't wake me.'

What was he twelve? Who needed their mum to wake them up? Sarah had stopped using her mum as a wakeup call way back in Primary School. He needed to grow up.

'Seriously?'

'I know it sounds silly but mother likes to wake me up with toast, tea and orange juice. She likes to still feel needed. But today she didn't, when I finally woke up she wasn't there! She had left a note, saying 'Out playing tennis', It is not my fault,' he insisted.

'Forget it, let's just get going.'

Arriving at 'Best Bites' just in the nick of time she looked over at him and he winked at her. Her stomach flipped. How could he do this to her. Her Hugh Grant wannabe was warming her heart yet again.

In the event she needn't have worried about his little boy act, he must save that for his mother. At the tasting he was nothing but charming to the company representative and loved all their suggestions and seemed pretty clued up about food. Must be all that fine dining those posh types do thought Sarah.

She made a note of what canapés he had preferred and added pricing to the side.

They thanked 'Best Bites' and left.

Back on the tube they sat down next to each other and she found his head falling onto her shoulder, she jolted him and told him to behave himself. Out came those eyes from behind the curtains and she realised that actually she didn't really mind if he used her as a head prop, as long as he had no intention of dribbling…

Tommy had said that he wanted to have a hog roast for the guests and so they were on their way to meet the two companies she had whittled down to. She was salivating at the thought of the tastings. Delicious, warm roasted pork in a bap oozing with apple sauce.

'Posh Pork' was their first stop. The name made Sarah giggle. Very apt for Mr Fawsett, posh by name and posh by nature. This was a real upper class outfit and the two ladies running the business had cut glass accents and said 'Yar' an awful lot. Unsurprisingly Tommy had an instant rapport with them and whispered to Sarah that he was convinced he had known one of them many years ago, through a friend of a friend.

'Camille, do you by any chance know Lucy and Philippa Davis Law?'

'Oh Yah, Tommy, they do sound famille, probs went to school with them.'

This time they got the bus to their next appointment and on the bus Tommy seemed really enthused by 'Posh Pork'.

'I loved their food Sarah. Delish wasn't it? The girls were such fun too and very profesh.' Praises were coming out of his every pore.

Sarah thought she had seen a spark between Tommy and the other partner in the company, Arabella. Of course there would be, they were like two peas in a pod. Very well suited. How had she ever thought that she had stood a chance with Tommy? He may well dabble in an alliance with her but she was evidently not settling down material to him. She knew nothing of his upbringing, lifestyle and set and wouldn't fit in coming from her own modest background.

Thankfully Camille and Arabella hadn't looked down at her but she was well aware of her limitations in being able to keep up with the Fawsetts. However, this was business and she was the paying customer as it were and so she felt perfectly happy with them and their company. As much as she didn't really want Tommy to have any contact with Arabella ever again she couldn't actually think of any reason why they shouldn't go with 'Posh Pork' for the hog roast.

She just agreed with Tommy and suggested waiting and seeing what the next company had to offer before making his mind up.

'Porkies' was up next and was a completely different set up. Run by a team of Essex based brothers Phil and Archie, they were renowned for their prize winning pigs and fun, almost barrow boy nature. Would this go down with the Hooray Henry Set?

They made Tommy laugh so much with their antics and showmanship. Sarah liked them a lot but decided that although they would be fabulous at any other event (she mentally made a note to add them to her best suppliers database) they were not the right fit for this themed event.

Outside Tommy was still laughing at what had gone on inside.

'Honestly Sarah, your job is so hard. How on earth do you choose who to go with?'

'Tommy, I am not going to lie to you, it is difficult but in this role you need to have a decisive nature. Decision making is one of my fortes,' Sarah lied.

'That is what I like about you Sarah. A strong,

independent woman.'

Tommy had her all wrong. Right now she didn't feel much like a strong, independent woman. Here she was seeing three men at the same time and not able to make a decision as to who she should ditch. Sarah had never been that good at making decisions, it was one of the reasons she had ended up taking the wrong subject choices at school. She just couldn't decide so just put them all in a hat and pulled out what would turn out to be the wrong ones. Why she had ever thought it would be a good idea to take geography when she couldn't stand forests was beyond her. Foreign languages were another such disaster, she just couldn't grapple with the correct pronunciation so her words came out all strained sounding like a strangled cat.

The last two calls of the day were to two dessert companies. These were going to be Sarah's favourite visits she could tell. She had a ridiculously sweet tooth and her stomach rumbled in happy anticipation at the thought of the tastings.

'Exquisite Desserts' was run by a delightful, motherly figure called Joan Spencer who specialised and trained in making pastries. No expense was spared at the tasting as she brought out trays of fruit tartlets and choux buns with fillings of dark chocolate and cherry, custard and sweet Chantilly cream.

She also promised she could do blackcurrant jellies in individual wine glasses in the party theme and to leave it to her and she would think up some other themed ideas exclusive to them. Both Sarah and Tommy could not help but get whipped up by her enthusiasm and were excited about the prospect of bespoke desserts.

'Crème De La Crème' was a more youthful company who had done their homework and had rang Alice and asked for more details about the event and so were ready and waiting with delectable sweet creations in the theme of the evening. Whilst not technically brilliant in taste compared to Joan's offerings Sarah wondered if the guests would even notice as by dessert time they would be full of alcohol..

Sarah decided to hold fire on making a decision on the desserts until Joan had sent over her themed ideas. She was confident that taste wise they would deliver, but did she have the right crowd in mind. Come to think of it, did Sarah have any idea what she was doing? If in doubt Tommy would guide her. She was sure he wouldn't set her up to fail.

CHAPTER ELEVEN

As Sarah came out of the tube her phone beeped – Answerphone message waiting from David. Oh crap, she had meant to call him and tell him it was over like she had promised Alice but it had completely slipped her mind.

'

'Sarah just listen' the message said. Then out of her phone an Elvis Presley tune played - You Are Always On My Mind.'

It made her think back to when she was a teenager and she had been watching The Elvis Story. Elvis had been away from home working away for a long time, returning home and being reunited with his family he had played it on the piano to his daughter, Lisa Marie. She had cried buckets at that then, she remembered with fond memories. It was the time she had spent far too long watching true made for TV films from America. Day after day she had tuned in to watch three part stories and films. In amidst the usual teenage angst and trials and tribulations, her emotions whacked her on the head in a way that caught her unawares and made her question her whole being. Love, Hurt, Jealousy and Revenge all featured.

She loved that song and the words were full of meaning and emotion. She started to cry. She felt like someone was literally pulling on her heart strings and it hurt, real bad. That was David, ever thoughtful but never there. She had been 'dating' him for far too long and wanted desperately for him to not have to go home in the middle of the night and just stay with her. She wanted to wake up with him beside her in her flat or even by now to have moved in with him, as it was all she got was the odd weekend away and that was supposed to be enough to placate her. While it had in the early days, it had been all fun and frolics then which she had liked. Life with David had been exciting and being whisked away for romantic getaways with an older, sophisticated man was terribly impressive, she had never once given a thought for the wife who had been left behind. In her head if the wife had been so nice then the man wouldn't need to stray. Yes, she had convinced herself that it was all Laura's fault, never mind that women like her had willingly gone with a married man knowing full well that they were most probably breaking another woman's heart in the process of getting their thrills.

Now however she felt like she was having a change of heart. How would Laura react when she found out, perhaps she already knew? What about the children, won't somebody think about the children.

She decided to keep the voicemail but wasn't going to

reply. She had to extricate herself and perhaps the easiest way would be to just ignore David and hope he got the message and went away.

She dialled Alice but got her answerphone, by now it was 6pm and it was too late to head back to the office.

She left a message – 'Alice, it's me. Just to let you know, meetings went well. Will fill you in tomorrow.'

Alice had deliberately ignored Sarah's phone call. Although she loved Sarah dearly, if Sarah was going to be a real partner in the business, and that was Alice's long term plans, she had to make herself unavailable at times. She wanted to see how she handled it and so far it was good.

Sarah seemed completely in control and relaxed when she left her messages.

Alice smiled at her dinner date. Perhaps she had finally found 'the one' too.

CHAPTER TWELVE

Next morning there was a text message from David on Sarah's phone.

'Sarah darling, are you ignoring me?'

And then five minutes later another came through.

'Sarah, I hope you are ok. Did you get my message?'

Sarah deleted them and walked into the office.

Alice looked up from her computer.

'Morning Sarah. Just to let you David called and left a

message, he asked you to call him.'

'Oh right, thanks,' Sarah replied airily. She waited for the question and then it came.

'Sarah I thought you were going to tell him it's over?'

'I did, he won't accept it,' Sarah lied.

'Oh, if he is causing you problems you could go to the police and get an injunction out on him. People do that you know. It's a thing,' Alice replied helpfully.

'Yes I will bear that in mind, shall we have that catch up meeting now?' Sarah tried to change the subject. The David issue could wait.

'Sarah that sounds brilliant,' Alice was pleased. The party plans sounded incredible. Sarah had taken to event planning like a duck to water.

'I agree with all the decisions you have made and you are completely right – 'Posh Pork' sounds exactly the right company for this particular event. Can you add Porkies to our database? They sound ace,' Alice made a note to go and visit them later that week.

At 11am a courier delivered some desserts from 'Exquisite Desserts' Sarah was surprised, she hadn't been expecting anything actually made from Joan. She had imagined just some descriptions of her ideas but here in its full glory was a box of delights. Sarah made some tea and took photos to share on Instagram. Alice had put her in charge of their social media and she realised that she had been neglecting it. She went through the pictures on her phone and found a few more food pics that would be suitable to share and some of her out and about at meetings and made a mental note to spend the afternoon making a concerted effort to tweet and Instagram. It would be great PR for the company.

Alice was busy devouring the desserts and with her mouth full said something that vaguely resembled 'These are good!' Sarah was surprised, Alice usually avoided sweet treats, it must be the time of the month.

'Joan is good, but as you know Crème De La Crème really embraced the type of event that we are planning. I just don't know who to go with Alice, it is such a hard decision!'

'Just call Joan and thank her for the delivery. Sleep on it tonight and let both companies know tomorrow Sarah.'

'But, if I don't know now, what is going to change by tomorrow?'

'I don't know,' Alice laughed. She realised she was not being particularly helpful but wanted Sarah to see that this job was not all fun food tastings and meetings. Sometimes you had to make tough decisions and let perfectly nice people down.

Unfortunately Sarah had been rather too good in sourcing and narrowing down the dessert companies, both were exceptional in their own ways and if truth be known, Alice would probably have just picked a name from a hat. Alice might intervene if she could see that Sarah was really stuck tomorrow but for now she wanted to see how Sarah handled her first real business dilemma.

After a late lunch Sarah started her social media onslaught. She noticed her food pictures were going down well and again looked through her phone to see if there were any more shareable images. As she flicked through she saw a picture of Tommy staring back at her. How on earth? She hadn't taken it so he must have. She giggled to herself. The guy was hilarious but she remained baffled as to how or why.

Her mobile started ringing, speak of the devil.

'Tommy! I was just looking at you.'

'Hello princess, say what?'

'A certain someone left a photo on my phone and I am looking at it right now, ring any bells?'

'Ah yes, so you got it?'

'Yes, I have. I am trying to work out how you did it. I am sure my phone has never left my side.'

'Well, I could tell you the secret but I would have to kill you.'

Dad, Tommy sounded just like her dad, except dad didn't possess that posh accent. She should call mum when she left work.

'Sarah, are you there?'

'Yes, sorry. You reminded me of something I need to do. Tommy, is there anything I can help you with?'

'Yes there was a reason for my call, as well as getting to listen to your sweet voice.'

Sarah didn't have a sweet voice so she knew that

Tommy was lying.

'I am going to have to bring the party forward.'

Sarah began to panic, her time lines were all planned with the original date in mind. How could he do this to her. Everything had been going so smoothly. She knew it had been too good to be true!

'Tommy, why?' She tried to sound composed but was aware of her voice wobbling.

'Oh a few invitees have decided to go on a Gap Year and they simply HAVE to be there, it's not a problem is it?'

Sarah wanted to scream at him 'Yes it is going to be a bloody problem! You have NO idea what it takes to plan a party of this size, you have NO concept of the real world. You think your money can just buy you anything you want, anytime you want it. Life doesn't work like that.'

She couldn't believe just for the sake of a few friends he wanted to change everything, she could cry. She really could. She hoped for her sake the chosen suppliers were going to be available for this new date or she would have to start all over again. She hated him.

'No it's not a problem.'

'Good, I knew it wouldn't be but I just wanted to check with you. Hey listen are you free tomorrow? I thought I would treat you to lunch. My favourite party planner,' he sounded so carefree. Completely unaware of just how much work he had potentially created for her. She of course couldn't let him know this however, instead she silently repeated the mantra 'The customer is always right!'

She kicked the dustbin under her desk and knocked it over, spilling the contents onto the carpet. Superb, more work.

'Can I get back to you tomorrow?' Right now she hated him but perhaps when she knew the level of her new workload and it wasn't quite as much as she had first thought, she might just thaw. Besides lunch was the least he could do after this little bombshell.

'Shit, shit, shit.'

'Everything OK Sarah?'

'Nah, Tommy has just moved all the goalposts, I feel a migraine coming on.'

'Sarah, work through it methodically. It might seem like the impossible right now but there is always a solution.

Believe me.'

'Well, if the Castle isn't available on this new date the whole event will be in jeopardy!'

'Not at all, just tell him he needs to up his budget and head to Europe! There are some stunning venues over there… I sense a European Fact Finding Mission on the horizon,' Alice winked at Sarah.

'Alice, I could kiss you! You are a genius,' Sarah hugged Alice. She instantly felt better. Of course, why hadn't she thought of it, he had plenty of money? She would simply get him to up his budget. Easy.

That afternoon she called Kendrick Castle.

'I am so sorry Sarah, we have a celebrity wedding on the date requested, ordinarily we would try to shift things around to fit all interested parties in but this is a no can do. I would love to tell you whose wedding it is but we are sworn to absolute secrecy,' Sarah had tried her best to find out who had booked the castle but to no avail. The battle-axe at the other end of the line was not budging. She must have had torture training by MI5, she was giving nothing away.

Kendrick Castle had been their first choice and whereas

a few hours before she may have been found crying into her coffee with despair, worried about letting the client down, after Alice's brainwave she was brimming with optimism.

She called round a few of her back up venues only to find to her relief that they too were apologising that they were booked up, this new date was after all slap bang in the middle of Wedding Season.

She called Tommy back.

'Hi Tommy, just to let you know I can make lunch tomorrow. See you then.'

CHAPTER THIRTEEN

'Move the party to somewhere in Europe?' Tommy looked shocked.

Sarah and Tommy were sat in a restaurant enjoying some succulent steak and drinking red wine. Things had been going very well until she had mentioned that she had a proposal for him regarding the event. This wasn't quite the reaction that Sarah had hoped for, she had always thought that rich types had no problem spending their money, right now, judging by his reaction, she may well have just said that Father Christmas wasn't real. He looked crestfallen.

'I am afraid so, it's our only hope if you want the party to go ahead. Your new date is slap bang in the middle of Wedding Season. I don't want to use the word impossible but if you want a 'wow' venue we don't have any alternative.'

'But that will push the price up.'

'It will indeed,' she wondered whether now was a good time to mention the trips abroad to view the three new venues she had googled and whittled down as possibilities.

'Are you absolutely sure there is no other way?'

'Oh trust me, I considered every alternative. This is not what I would have chosen…but look on the bright side, this way we have the potential to get coverage in the European press.'

He thought about it for a moment 'Hmmm, isn't that really an advantage for you? Doesn't really help me.'

She picked up a thrice baked chip and popped it in her mouth. He looked at her a little salaciously and smiled.

He suddenly perked up as if a light bulb had lit up his head 'Sarah, you are the expert, let's do it!'

Sarah breathed with relief, now was the perfect time to mention the trips abroad.

'There is something else.'

'Yes?'

'We haven't done an overseas event yet and so we are not totally au fait with these European venues. The thing is… we are going to need to fly over and visit them.'

'Absolutely fine. When shall we go?'

Good. He seemed keen. She guessed he wouldn't mind this being added to the overall budget.

'We?'

'Yes, you don't think I am going to let you travel alone now do you? Besides a few romantic jaunts are just what the both of us need right now.'

'Is that so?' She teased.

'Sarah, whatever you may think of me, I am not completely stupid. I know that by changing the original date I gave you an almighty headache so yes I do think that this would be a great idea.'

Sarah resigned herself to the idea that Tommy would be tagging along. She would have to run this by Alice. Secretly however she was looking forward to a little break, albeit a working one!

The steak was melting in her mouth, the chips were to die for and the red wine so smooth, slipping down her throat a little too easily. For a working lunch she could think of no nicer a place to be. This would make a fabulous venue for a date she thought.

They ended their meal with two coffees. There was no way she would have been able to have had dessert. The food had been delicious but incredibly rich and she still had to complete an afternoon of work back at the office.

'I will be in touch with some flight dates and suggestions Tommy. Thanks for lunch.'

'It's my pleasure entirely,' he placed his hand on the hollow of her back and led the way out of the restaurant. His touch sent a surge of electricity through her body. That little tingle stayed with her for the rest of the afternoon.

Alice was at her desk when she got back. Her head was being supported by her hand and she had this strange sort of grin painted on her face.

'Everything OK Alice?'

'Hmmm? Yes of course…why?'

'You just seem miles away, to be honest you haven't been all there for a while now.'

'Haven't I? Well sorry for being in love.'

'WHAT?? Details! What is his name? Where did you meet? Spill the beans!'

'All in good time. I don't want to jinx it. Besides it is early days. So tell me about lunch. Is he up for the change of plan?'

'Absolutely. Not a problem at all. Only thing is he wants to come on the fact finding mission with me. I wasn't sure if that was the done thing?'

'Well two bedrooms will of course push the cost up, however he is the client. He should have an input in the decision if he wants to and it sounds like it does. Can you handle him?'

'Who Tommy? Of course! Ha ha honestly Alice.

Sometimes he acts just like a big kid.'

'Don't they all?'

'Although I have to say at lunch today he seemed to show me a different, more grown up version of Tommy.'

'Oh by the way. David called again. He didn't mention that you two had split?'

'Like I said, he won't accept it.'

Damn. She really should call him Sarah thought.

Instead she called her mum and got an update on her dad. She told her mum that she was planning to go away for a few days on a business trip but promised to visit Dad before she went. Her dad had been making good progress her mum reassured her. He would hopefully be out of the hospital in a week or so all things being well. Sarah was pleased. Her mum and dad made such a good team she didn't know how either of them would cope if and when they lost the other.

Her phone beeped.

A text from Adam. Oh my goodness! In her attempt at not appearing too keen she had completely forgotten to reply to his last text. Eek!

'Hey sad girl. I haven't heard from you in a while. Well actually I haven't heard from you at all. Are you still up for meeting up again? No problem if not. Just need to know where I stand'

How was he so nice when she had ignored him? If it had been the other way round and she hadn't heard from him she would have just chalked it up to him not being interested and deleted his number!

She replied straightaway 'Sorry, things have been a bit hectic this end. Yes of course!'

'Marvellous. You know you are my favourite girl :)'

'Going to be away for a few days on business. Will text you to arrange a date for when I get back. OK?'

'Are you sure it's just business? ;-)'

Did he know something Sarah wondered? He couldn't possibly unless he was stalking her… perhaps he wasn't so nice after all, his good looks could be deceiving her. She shook her head, she really shouldn't watch Crimewatch when home alone.

'Yes what else would it be?'

'Ooh defensive! I was just teasing. Enjoy your trip. Yours waiting until you return, Adam x'

Adam put his phone down. Sarah was a hard woman to pin down. From that first meeting he had felt something he had never felt before. He knew she must be something special and something was making him return to her and want more. He wasn't sure she felt the same way yet or indeed if she ever would but he owed it to fate to try.

The director spoke 'Adam, we are ready for you on set.'

He hurried back 'Sorry!' He turned to the camera and side on smouldered into it. Click, click, click went the camera.

'And we are done!'

Adam left the building and headed down to Old Street on the tube. He wasn't in the habit of stalking women, he just wanted to see her face again. He stood in a doorway and watched her leave the office. She really was so beautiful.

He went to walk in the opposite direction when he became aware of some commotion in front of Sarah. An older man was holding a huge bunch of flowers and on bended knee was singing at the top of his voice. A crowd had gathered. He hurried over being careful to be just out of view of the two of them.

'Get up David, you are embarrassing me!' Sarah hissed.

David ignored her and continued singing Smokey Robinson's 'Tracks Of My Tears'

'Sarah my love. Why won't you answer my calls? I am crazy about you,' he started up again.

'David please stop it!' She begged him, she then looked for an escape route but the crowd had surrounded them in a ring of steel.

Someone called out 'He loves you! Have a heart, Lady!'

She could hear mutterings of 'How sweet' from women and similar nice quotes echoing around her. Yes well you wouldn't think that if you knew he was married with kids she thought. I bet you would tell me not to touch him with a barge pole.

She had had quite enough.

'David, I am asking you one last time. Please stop this hideous public display.'

She hated attention at the best of times and here she was in the centre of a spectacle she wanted nothing to do with.

She began to regret not calling him back earlier and letting him down gently. This way was going to be much worse for both of them.

Sarah. I will do ANYTHING, anything I mean it! You just say it. Being apart from you has made me realise what I am missing. I want us to be together forever,' He was off singing again, this time Rick Astley's 'Together Forever'.

Sarah rolled her eyes and a few people started to walk away.

Adam looked on in confusion. He felt hurt. Sarah had lied to him, he had asked her if she was single and she had told him yes. Yet here was this David guy professing undying love right before his very eyes. They obviously had history.

He turned around and walked away. He had just wanted a peek of Sarah, waiting for her to return felt like it was going to be too long. Nothing good could come of stalking her, he had got more than he bargained for. At least he knew the truth now.

Sarah edged closer to David and snatched the flowers off of him.

'Get up!' She snapped at him.

David was shocked, he had never heard that tone come from Sarah before.

'Let's go for a drink,' she suggested.

He stood up and dusted off his knees. The pavement had been cold and now his trousers felt wet. David didn't know what had come over him but he just knew this lady was the love of her love and he was going to fight for her and do everything in his power to keep her.

Sarah glared at the bystanders still watching them. 'OK you can go home now, nothing to see here.'

A man patted David on the shoulders 'Good luck mate, she is a stunner.'

Sarah marched ahead of David. This was not how she had planned to spend her evening.

'Shall I grab us a seat?'

'No thanks, I am not staying long.'

'David, there is no easy way to say this so I am just going to come out and say it. Things haven't been right for a while now, it's over.'

'What? But, no. This cannot be happening! Sarah I have been doing a lot of thinking. I knew things had to change and so I did it.'

'You did what?'

'I told Laura, I told her all about us. I told her I was leaving her. My marriage is over.'

'Oh,' Sarah wanted to care, she really did. But this David before her was not the man she had fallen for. Standing before her was a broken, sad man. She couldn't go back now. It was not what she wanted.

'David. I am sorry. I am afraid I meant every word. I am moving on and I suggest you do the same.'

'Sarah, please. This is crazy. I know you love me and I love you. Let's give it a shot?'

Gah, why wouldn't he accept it. She had to think fast. This had to be final.

'David, it won't work. I have met someone else.'

David started to quietly sob.

'You are making a big mistake. No one will love you more than me, no one.'

'I will take that chance,' she just wanted to leave now.

'But, I have nowhere to go. Laura threw me out there and then. Sarah please?' He was desperate.

'David. Is that what you really wanted me for? A room

for the night? You earn enough money. Get a hotel room.'

'Goodbye David.'

She walked out of the bar, handing the bunch of flowers to a couple just entering.

'I hope these make you happy.'

CHAPTER FOURTEEN

Tommy arrived at Sarah's flat at 5.30am in the morning all bright and cheery.

'Are you ready? The taxi is waiting.'

Sarah was all dressed up in her business suit and high heel ankle straps. The heels may have been ultra-thin and precarious looking but she was used to walking in them and felt sturdy enough even if she appeared to be teetering on the brink. She grabbed her pull along case (who ever invented these was a genius) and closed the door behind her.

They sat in the taxi, knees touching. Her skirt had slid up and she had a lot of leg on show. She found his hands wandering and quickly pushed them away.

'Don't get any ideas.'

After the rather messy events of the other night she was swearing herself off men for the time being and whereas she may have found Tommy's behaviour charming before, right now it was irritating her. Perhaps she just needed some more sleep.

Tommy put his hands up 'Sorry! It's just that you are so very tempting, particularly at this time of the morning.'

'Please, don't men think about ANYTHING else?'

Tommy looked dejected.

'From now on I will be on my best behaviour,' he promised.

He was wearing a t-shirt, a pair of converse trainers and some slouchy jeans. She in her power suit looked the complete opposite. She did feel a little overdressed but this was a business trip and she was representing the company and besides had she dressed down she may not have approached the trip in the same way. She did need a holiday so it would have been all too easy to slip into holiday mode.

They sat in silence for the rest of the journey.

The taxi dropped them off at the departures terminal. Sarah was lagging behind. Perhaps the heels were a little too high after all. It was one thing to wear them in the office where she was sat down all day but quite another when you had to walk miles around an airport just to get to the departure gate.

'I see you are appropriately dressed,' Tommy's eyes fell down to her heels. 'If you think I am going to carry your case for you, you are very much mistaken.'

'I am not asking you to, I can manage thanks,' Sarah retorted. Whatever happened to chivalry she thought and whatever happened to his charm. It seemed like he was punishing her for rejecting his advances.

After security, she had a look around Duty Free whilst Tommy hung around outside. The staff on the counters kept pouncing on her so she found herself agreeing to items she had no interest in – the latest green nail polish anyone? After walking around a few times she managed to resist temptation and put back the basket of beauty goodies she had picked up to the dismay of the sales assistants. She smiled sweetly at them and said 'I forgot my flight ticket, I'll be back.'

Tommy had disappeared so she wandered in and out of the shops looking for him and eventually found him in Pret sipping a coffee. She ordered a Mocha and joined him.

'Buy anything nice? You were gone ages.'

'I have spent most of the time looking for you if you must know. You could have said where you were going! And no, I didn't buy anything.'

The mix of chocolate and coffee was hitting the spot nicely. She found herself relaxing, perhaps she had just needed a caffeine fix.

Her phone beeped. A text from Alice.

'Have a good trip. Keep in touch x'

They looked up at the departures board, their flight was flashing – 'NOW BOARDING – FINAL CALL'.

Shit! How had that happened? They had arrived in plenty of time and so of course neither of them had been keeping an eye on the time. They grabbed their things and started running and running and running. Not easy in heels. Typical, they had to get to the furthest away gate in Olympic Record time. There was no way they were going to make it.

By the time they had reached the gate they were red in the face and Sarah could barely breathe. However, no one was boarding, everyone was just sat down waiting in an even smaller area and there was no one manning the desk. Final call my arse, Sarah vowed never to be taken in again by this little trick from the airline.

Soon they were ready to board and going down the stairs to the plane two men wearing suits noticed Sarah struggling to negotiate the stairs in heels whilst carrying her case. Tommy was walking a little ahead, completely oblivious to her predicament.

'Can we help you with that bag?'

'Oh that is very kind of you but I can manage.'

Tommy heard this exchange, ashamed he waltzed back to her and without saying anything whisked up the case into his hands. For the rest of the trip he carried her bag. Chivalry had returned.

Sarah smiled and said nothing. Shamed by the two men she thought. That will teach him.

Back in the office Alice took a call from David.

'Can I speak to Sarah please?'

'David, she isn't here.'

'Where is she?'

'I am afraid I can't tell you, staff confidentiality.'

'Don't be so ridiculous,' David was desperate, he needed to speak to Sarah, to see her. He had been thinking hard since the singing incident and had decided that he should propose. If she had any doubts as to his future intentions this would bury it once and for all.

He had chosen and bought a ring from Tiffany & Co in anticipation. Sarah had often spoken about the kind of ring she liked and had mentioned her dream ring would be found inside the famous blue box. He just needed to get her to agree to meet him. He had it all planned out, drinks at The Savoy, the backdrop of The Beaufort Bar. He would order her a cocktail and then he would go down on bended knee and hand her the blue box. She would have tears in her eyes as she saw the box, and melt into his arms as she accepted his proposal.

Alice put the phone down. This guy really wouldn't let it go. She was thanking her lucky stars that her new man was single and came with no baggage. After her experience with a married man there was nothing on earth that would make her go back there, ever.

Alice pulled up a spreadsheet and took a look at the company's figures. Things were going well, so well in fact she wondered if she should be taking on more staff. Sarah had embraced her project with enthusiasm and vigour and was proving herself to be trustworthy. If only she knew that Tommy had specifically asked for her to deal with his event and at that point she hadn't even worked for 'Perfect Events'.

Unbeknown to Sarah, Tommy had spotted her in a nightclub that Alice and Sarah had been dancing in. They had had a 'no men' rule girl's night out that evening. Sarah had adhered to it but Alice had fallen off the waggon when Tommy's friend Alexander had approached her on the way to the toilets. He had been quite persistent so making sure that Sarah was nowhere to be seen she had a quick snog with him and now here they were, together a few month's down the line.

Tommy had wandered over and asked Alice who her friend was. Alice extricated herself from them but not before Alexander had got hold of her phone and added his number to it.

'Where have you been?' Sarah quizzed Alice.

'Queue for the toilet was long!' Alice lied.

After that every time she looked around she had noticed these two guys looking at them. Sarah didn't seem to notice though which Alice was relieved about.

No more than a few days had passed before she got a text from Tommy asking to be put in touch with her friend and if not then he would have to employ her to do his event and could she possibly put the friend in charge.

She was going to reply and say that Sarah didn't work for her but then Sarah had been made redundant. Alice had wanted the business so the natural step had been to ask Sarah to join her.

Alice laughed. Sneaky maybe but if Tommy was anything like Alex who was such a lovely guy then it would be a match made in heaven and a few years down the line she could retell her amazing match making story at Tommy and Sarah's wedding to great applause.

Except Tommy was nothing like the sophisticated and mature Alex. He was far more immature and seemingly unready for the kind of grown up relationship that Sarah needed and deserved right now.

Back on the plane Tommy and Sarah ordered some breakfast and he seemed to have put the recent rejection of his advances to the back of his mind. He was looking forward to spending some time with Sarah away from their usual environment.

He didn't often slum it on a budget airline as most of his friends hired private jets but this was quite a lot of fun. The seats were tightly packed together and so there was barely any room for him to stretch his legs out. He felt rather claustrophobic and was wriggling about a bit until Sarah snapped at him.

'Do you have to do that? Sit still, you are making my iPad shake.'

Sarah had had her head buried deep in her iPad, she figured if she pretended she was hard at work she wouldn't have to talk to him more than necessary. She flicked through her updated presentation. Pleasingly all the suppliers could work with the new dates and were happy to travel abroad, paid for of course.

She had eventually decided to go with Crème De La Crème for desserts, they had sealed the deal by calling the next day and offering a little more for the money she was prepared to pay. Calling Joan back and letting her down had been hard but she thought it better to speak to her rather than email her with the 'It's a no' news. Joan had been very gracious and Sarah had reassured her that the quality of her work was not in question and that she had been added to their preferred Supplier database which made Joan really happy.

Sarah went through and familiarised herself with their European Trip agenda. She had narrowed it down to three castles in three beautiful countries.

First stop – Germany

Second Stop – Italy

Final Stop – France

Three spectacular castles – she made some notes on the things she would be looking out for and the questions she would ask each of them. She would then be able to do a direct comparison on pros and cons. She was a strong believer in gut feeling so wasn't going to discount that either. Of course Tommy may well have his own preference and when it came down to it as long as all the pieces of the puzzle fitted together then ultimately he would have the final choice.

She started to feel really tired, she glanced over at Tommy who had now settled down with his ear phones in his ear listening to music and closed her eyes.

'Wake up, we are here,' she felt Tommy tapping her shoulders.

She must have fallen asleep. She stretched out and shook away her sleep.

'Wow, I must have been tired!'

'Did you have any nice dreams, was I in them?'

Sarah ignored him and got her case down from the overhead locker. Entering Germany was far easier than going through security to leave England and soon they were outside and waiting for their taxi, she had a look around for a white card with her name on it. She had ordered the taxi before they had left England so that they didn't waste any time as their schedule was tight.

She had planned to head straight to the first venue to take a look around and then head back to their hotel later in the afternoon to check in. In her experience the rooms were never ready anyway and this seemed like a much better use of time.

Tommy's enthusiasm wasn't wavering.

'I have never been to Germany, have you Sarah?'

'No, never come to think of it.'

Sarah had been to quite a few countries in her life and

yet she realised that she had never been to Germany. She had had it on her to visit list for a few years now as she had quite fancied taking in one of their famous Christmas markets. She couldn't think of any other reason to visit though if she was telling the truth.

They drove through wild countryside with not a sound coming from the front of the car, if she wasn't witnessing the driver actually driving she would have wondered if he was dead. The sun was fast disappearing under a cover of clouds. The white clouds made way for dark rain clouds and soon rain was belting against the car windows. Sarah desperately wanted to open a window, the heat was stifling and she was starting to feel sick.

She noticed that the car was so old it had wind down handles for the back windows, relieved she rolled her side down a small way. She didn't care that it was letting in some rain. The fresh air was welcoming and finally she could breathe again. She hoped that whoever was showing them round the castle was able to provide her with a biscuit or two and a cup of tea. Her stomach was rumbling and she realised that in her meticulous planning she had forgotten to factor in food stops.

'There it is!' Tommy yelled a little too enthusiastically as they both looked on towards a huge and imposing brick building fast approaching them.

It certainly had an eeriness that was befitting the theme Tommy had chosen and it hadn't been too far from the airport, all bonuses that Sarah made a mental note of.

She had hired the taxi for the day so they had no worries about cost or timings. The driver would be staying in the grounds until she gave him the signal that they were ready to leave.

A smart woman with her hair in a bun and dressed all in black greeted them at the front.

'Guten Tag Frau Dawes, Herr Fawsett. Wilkommen, wilkommen, Sprechen Sie Deutsch?'

Sarah had briefly studied German for a year way back when she was thirteen. She understood the lady standing in front of her but there was no way her German was up to scratch to carry out a whole conversation in it, she hoped for both their sake's she spoke English.

'Danke Schon, do you speak English? I am afraid my German is very limited.'

'Of course!' Please come this way,' she said in her German accent.

Sarah noticed Tommy had remained silent, if he could speak German he wasn't letting on. They followed the lady who introduced herself as Frau Jung. She led the way to a sitting room and Sarah was grateful to see some food - traditional cakes and biscuits - laid out and a hot steaming pot of tea ready and waiting for them.

'You must be hungry after your journey, please sit down. It is just a small something before we take a look around.'

This must be the famous hospitality that the Germans were known for. Sarah was warming to Frau Jung. The cakes were delicious and the tea quickly warmed them up. The castle was quite chilly Sarah noted.

'This of course is a private room. For the purposes of event hire we allow guests to mingle freely in the grounds outside, you may put a marquee up if you require it. We have a preferred supplier list should you need to see it. You will also have access to two rooms inside the castle plus we have a catering kitchen for use, if necessary. One room is the ball room, we anticipate this to be where the main event is held and a smaller room where guests can retire to from the fun and noise…'

They stood up and followed Frau Jung's lead. They walked through corridors until they arrived at two huge thick doors and she pulled out an enormous key to open them.

Inside it opened up to reveal the most incredible room Sarah had ever seen – the ceilings were high and gigantic crystal chandeliers were hanging down from them. They must have cost an absolutely fortune she thought. The room was a perfect rectangle which would make things easier for layout. She wondered whether the band would bring a temporary stage, she felt that if they didn't they would get lost in the room's vastness. She looked over at Tommy. He was making his way around the room taking it all in she hoped. The circular tables were laid out in mock party style.

'I took the liberty of preparing the room in the style we would prefer it to be laid out. We find this gives potential guests a good idea of what it can look like, so you don't have to imagine if you like. I hope you don't mind.'

It was all very grand and this was just perfect. She wondered if Tommy felt the same. She reminded herself that there were two other potential venues to see before making a decision.

'No, not at all. It is very helpful to us. Thank you.'

Sarah went through her list of questions and made a note of all the answers in her specially created comparison spreadsheet.

She called the taxi to say that they were ready to be picked up and thanked Frau Jung for showing them around and promised she would be in touch before next week.

Once back in the taxi she finally broke the silence.

'Well, what do you think?'

'I liked it. A lot. I wonder though if it may just be a bit too big for what we need but I loved that Frau Jung was pretty relaxed about our plans.'

He yawned. 'I think I may give dinner a miss tonight if you don't mind. I am feeling tired. Before you say anything, may I remind you I was up earlier than you AND I wasn't the one who slept on the plane.'

'Fair enough,' Sarah wasn't about to argue with him.

Sarah wondered if ordering room service was allowed as she had never sat in a restaurant all by herself but in the event thought there was a first time for anything, however she changed her mind and went down for dinner in the hotel restaurant alone.

She ordered a coke, although she liked wine like the best of them she was most definitely a social drinker and found she only really enjoyed it in the company of others. She wandered around the buffet choosing plenty of salad and some fish, and then some slices of hot meat, chips and rice. She was very hungry, Tommy was really missing out. The selection was really quite wonderful. She did note however that bar some fresh fruit in a bowl and a tray with a selection of cheeses there didn't appear to be any desserts. Disappointing.

She turned on her phone to find a text waiting from Adam.

'Hey, how's the business trip going? Not too boring I hope x'

Sweet, sweet Adam. She should call him as soon as she got back to England. There was real potential in that relationship she thought. Of course it was very early days but she felt that they had really clicked and she wanted to get to know him more.

'Hi, thanks for the text! I guess you can't get me out of your mind eh? Business trip so so. They aren't all glamourous you know. I am currently sat eating dinner alone! X'

Was she flirting with him, she wasn't sure but this was fun. She hoped she came across as self-assured. He was so good looking he needed taking down a peg or two, besides it was nice to be chased by a gorgeous guy for once!

She sipped her coke and smiled to herself. She wondered how long it would take for him to reply, the answer was not very long at all. Her phone beeped back at her almost immediately.

'You poor thing! x' So, Adam thought, she must be telling the truth, this was a business trip after all and not a romantic getaway with her lover.

When he had walked away the other night he had run the events of that night over and over in his head. That David guy sure seemed keen but when he thought about it Sarah hadn't looked so keen. Perhaps she was telling the truth and she was single. He hoped so. He was tired of flying all over the world with no one waiting for him when he got home. He knew he was good looking and most guys would probably be jealous of him and his lifestyle but it was a lonely life. He got a lot of attention from women but because he was particularly good looking they didn't seem to want to have a relationship with him in case he left them for someone else. All he needed was a woman to put her heart on the line. He would prove to them that it wasn't all about appearances and deep down all he wanted was to have that special someone to share life with.

Her phone beeped again, this time it was her mum.

'Sarah darling, good news. Dad should be out very soon. He asked after you today. We all miss you. Mum'

And then another came through – Using the hotel's WI FI was obviously paying off.

'Sarah, Mum isn't coping at all well. She might be trying to keep up a brave face but I hear her sobbing into her pillow every night. Can you call me when you get back? I think you may need to pay us another visit'

Sarah felt her stomach lurch. Family problems. Her mum's text had been so upbeat, and yet Charlotte's was filled with doom and gloom. She put away thoughts of home until she really had to think about them again.

'Dessert madam?' The waiter stood there holding a menu 'We make them to order'.

She was impressed. She couldn't finish the evening without a dessert. She was worried about her parents and she needed some sweet comfort food.

'Oh yes please,' taking the menu her eyes jumped across the words.

'I recommend the Schwarzwälderkirschtorte – You may know it better by the English name – 'Black Forest Gateaux.' It was always good to try the national dishes when in the country.

'Then I shall have that, thank you,' she really should ask the serving staff more often for their recommendations, it sure did make it easier to make a decision.

Black Forest Gateaux…she hadn't had it for years! She remembered it fondly as the birthday cake of choice for a while with her family. She loved the mix of chocolate and cherries. She was going to enjoy this.

The waiter reappeared with a huge slice of cake and Sarah ordered a coffee to accompany it. Just then Tommy sauntered towards her table.

Grinning he said 'Just in time for a night cap, hope you haven't missed me too much.'

The waiters had been packing away the buffet food but offered to make up a plate up for him which he agreed would be nice if it wasn't too much trouble. He asked for some cheese and fruit, far healthier than her option. Sarah glanced down at her plate full of chocolate sponge, whipped cream and cherries, he may have made a healthier choice but this was the much better choice.

'Ooh cheese before bed, a brave choice!' She ribbed him.

'Is it?' Not getting the joke she noticed, she wasn't sure she could be bothered to explain.

'Never mind.'

'No, tell me. Why is it a brave choice?'

'Oh it's just that they say if you have cheese before bed it gives you nightmares,' Sarah wondered where this conversation was heading.

'Oh really? I always have cheese before bed. I have never noticed. Mind you I can't actually remember if I do dream at all the next morning. My mind wakes up completely blank.'

He tucked into his humongous mountain of food. It seemed that the waiters had no idea what he would have selected so had placed everything that had been on offer on the plate.

Sarah had laughed when it had arrived but Tommy had no problems polishing it off within seconds.

He wiped his mouth on his sleeve 'That was good, I was starving!'

'In that case you were lucky to come down when you did, you almost missed it.'

'Yes well I thought you would wake me.'

'You said you wanted to sleep. I was respecting your decision. I am not a mind reader,' Sarah was irritated, it wasn't her job to manage his life as well as her own. He really needed to grow up.

'Early start tomorrow, I take it you will be wanting me to get you up so you don't miss breakfast before we head to the airport?'

'That would be great.'

'I am going to head up now, see you tomorrow,' she wanted to leave before he did so that they didn't have an awkward parting at her hotel room door. She had a feeling he may try to wheedle his way into her room and she wanted to avoid it if she could.

He let her go. Tommy sat there eating his cheese and biscuits. He watched her wiggle in her high heels as she walked away from him. This girl was so hot she was sizzling he thought. He felt movement in his trousers and took a swig of his vodka. Yet her charm seemed to be that she had absolutely no idea just what a catch she was.

He thought he may introduce her to the family when

they got back to England. Although technically they were working together on the event, on the night he wanted her to be his girlfriend. There was plenty of time for her to thaw out and succumb to his charms. He loved how organised she was, just like mummy he thought. His dad hadn't been good at running the family estate but his mum was so good at it that she had taken one look at the finances and launched a PR and Marketing offensive where she opened up the grounds to the public for a small fee.

Sarah, Tommy thought, based on what he had seen was just the sort of girl that would be able to take on the task of running Fawsett House and be just as successful at it once his parent's had passed away. Yes there was no doubt in his mind Sarah was the one for him. She just didn't know it yet.

His phone beeped. It was a text from Arabella. She was a cutie, his parents would love her too. He wondered if it was ok to marry Sarah but have a bit of Arabella on the side. After all if it was OK for the future King of England…

'Tommy, Dahling. Party at mine at the weekend. Bring a bottle x'

Arabella had made it plain she was interested in Tommy. After their first meeting she had called him drunk in the middle of the night from a nightclub to tell him she had sent a taxi over to bring him to her. He had arrived to find her draped across a private table, a magnum of Champagne and two glasses in her hands.

'You came!' She snogged him hard before he could wrestle her off. Still he couldn't deny she was pretty hot and possessed the longest legs he had ever seen. No harm in keeping his options open he thought. Yes he liked Sarah but she had yet to show much real interest in him. Arabella however was there for the taking and in his eyes that was a rather attractive quality right now.

CHAPTER FIFTEEN

Next morning Sarah was in a much better mood having had plenty of sleep. She dialled Tommy's room.

'Good morning. This is your early wakeup call.'

'Mmm, so nice to hear your voice this early in the morning,' Tommy murmured dreamily.

'Downstairs in ten.'

She was already tucking into her breakfast buffet when he arrived. Sarah usually had a small bowl of porridge with blueberries every morning but when it came to a Hotel's breakfast buffet she found it all too easy to over indulge. She opted for a coffee, pancakes, maple syrup and a bit of fresh fruit. Another plate contained scrambled eggs, toast and grilled tomatoes. She justified it by telling herself it could be ages before their next stop and if she didn't eat too often she could get travel sick.

If she thought that she had overdone it she soon realised it was nothing to what was on Tommy's plate. This guy could eat for England. He had the full works on his and told her that that was just Round 1. If she worried that she was going to be sick from a lack of eating, she was concerned that he would be sick from overeating.

She also noted that he had downed 4 black coffees in the time she had sipped her milky, sweet coffee. Off he jumped up to get Round 2 as he called it, this time he had moved onto the pastries and toast. Round 3 consisted of fruit and yoghurt.

'Right, I am done,' he finally declared.

Sarah was feeling a bit woozy from the sight of all the food he had just consumed.

'Good. We have to check out, the airport calls. Look out Italy, we are coming to get you.'

This time they made their plane with plenty of time to spare. European airports were so much smaller and easier to navigate thought Sarah. She noticed Tommy engrossed in his phone, she wondered what was so entertaining. He looked up to see her looking at him.

'Can't keep your eyes off me huh?'

'You wish!'

Sarah settled into her window seat and drifted off, soon she found herself dreaming of Adam. She woke up feeling a bit disorientated and disconcerted. Her dream was far too graphic and steamy for her liking, what a relief it had just been a dream. She opened her eyes to see if anyone had noticed to find Tommy's face virtually on top of hers.

She sat up straight and attempted to look composed. He wasn't having any of it.

'You OK there? That must have been some dream, you looked like you were having a lot of fun there!'

Sarah was absolutely mortified, could she appear to be anything less than professional after this little episode.

'Hmmm…? I have no idea what you mean. Are we set to land anytime soon?'

He grinned at her 'Oh yah of course, they say we forget

dreams as soon as we wake up, well except nightmares which can stay with us for years.'

Sarah wondered who 'they' were but she carried on with the pretence of feigning ignorance.

'Oh by the way... Who is Adam?' he asked.

'Adam?' Oops, so now she was aware that not only was she acting out her dreams she was also talking in them. Wonderful, just wonderful. Not very professional in front of the client.

She wished the earth would swallow her up right there and then but sadly it didn't so she excused herself and nipped to the toilet to freshen up in preparation for landing. Hand cream rubbed into her hands, lip salve applied to her lips and a spritz on the face of her Avene Soothing and Hydrating Mist and a squirt or three of her Philosophy 'Amazing Grace' perfume soon had her sorted and calm, ready to face the world and Tommy again.

Sarah stood up ready to get off of the plane and as Tommy leaned in to reach up and bring down their cases she leant out and felt his face brush against her neck.

'Mmm, you smell nice,' he murmured in appreciation.

Sarah felt confused, he seemed to be playing games with her. One minute he was all over her, the next he was pulling away. A sign of immaturity, stay away Sarah she warned herself. He didn't know what he wanted and she was tired of all these games. If he wanted her he needed to lay down his cards and let her know properly.

She imagined how she would say this to his face and then decided that perhaps she didn't want to overcomplicate things with a business client, she had tried dating a colleague and that hadn't worked so why on earth would this relationship.

Besides she had dreamt of Adam which had to be her subconscious telling her something. He appeared to be a strong believer in fate, perhaps she should now let fate take control and send her in the right direction too.

The Italian security guards perked up when they saw Sarah walk up to passport control nudging each other and giving knowing looks.

'La mia bella signora,' the official smiled at Sarah and waved her through. 'Ciao,' he made her turn back to look at him.

She recognised the word bella and signora as meaning beautiful lady and smiled back. This was Italy, the romantic country, she had only been on their soil for a few minutes and already she was being wooed by the men. They were living up to their reputation as Casanovas and she wasn't minding it one little bit.

She looked around to find Tommy who had gone into another queue and noticed that he was still there.

She watched as the officials looked him up and down and sneered at him.

'You look, how you say, messy. In Italy we like to dress well,' she heard one of them tell him.

She laughed as he walked through. He didn't look too happy.

'I like the way I dress, it may be shabby but it IS designer shabby,' he reassured her.

'Oh I wouldn't worry. If you are happy then who are they to take that away from you?'

He noticed she hadn't complimented him on his appearance. Perhaps he should think about growing up and changing his style. He noted that they had a spare day in Rome, he would surprise Sarah. He felt that he was losing her interest, he would show her just how mature he could be. Sarah he could tell wanted a real man. He could be that man. The charm offensive had to be ramped up if he was to get the girl.

They headed into the centre of Rome to their hotel by taxi. They were viewing the castle the next day so had an afternoon and evening to themselves. Tommy wanted to ask Sarah what her plans were and Sarah was thinking the same. Should they spend the day together sightseeing, Sarah was tempted to take in a couple of the sights if there was time and she didn't really fancy doing it alone in one of the world's most romantic cities.

She went to ask him just as he spoke at the same time.

'You first!' He proffered.

'OK, I was just wondering when we drop our bags at the hotel do you want to head out for some sightseeing with me, that is unless you already have plans?'

'You won't believe this but I was just about to say the same thing!'

'That's settled then,' she smiled at him.

The hotel was beautiful, all old world glamour and plenty of dark wood. The bed was huge and comfortable.

Sarah turned on her phone, hoping she wasn't about to find a family crisis looming, a text from David or and she hated to admit this, a text or voicemail from Alice. For today only.

****

Alice had woken up entwined in the arms of Alexander, it was 9am and she noticed that her phone was beeping. Three missed calls and a matching number of voicemails. Business was booming, love was in the air, life was pretty perfect at this moment. She wished she could bottle it up and keep it forever as it was bound to change. After the incident with the married lecturer she had lost faith in life ever coming together for her again and she had held a huge mistrust of men. Slowly but surely dating Alexander was showing her that all men were not the same. She had stayed over with Alexander in his Knightsbridge flat last night and she was looking forward to her journey into work on a bus. The beauty of her business was that she wasn't just tied to the office, she could pretty much work anywhere. She decided to make a lazy morning of it, Alexander had a fabulously large bar in the centre of his kitchen that was ideal for drinking coffee on whilst working through her emails.

Tonight she was overseeing an event and would be up late so she figured a lazy morning was the trade-off.

His place also had floor to ceiling windows that on this wonderfully clear morning allowed her to enjoy incredible views of the city. She loved London and knew she would never, ever leave.

She took a picture, logged onto Instagram and added the photo with the caption 'The view from my office this morning 'and instantly she received notification of 10 likes. She added some relevant hashtags and watched the like count grow. She noticed that Sarah had been busy too, adding a few pictures of Germany and the potential party venue. The Instagram account was gaining followers by the day and this in turn was bringing the company to the attention of a wider audience.

She decided not to contact Sarah, there was no need to keep asking for updates or ask her if she needed help. Sarah would ask if she needed it, she had never shied away from asking for assistance.

Alexander had popped out and returned with some freshly baked, still warm croissants and they ate these with their vat sized mugs of coffee. He cuddled her and she in turn hugged him back.

'So how are the two love birds?' Alexander asked.

'I have no idea, I haven't heard from Sarah. Have you heard from Tommy at all?'

'Nope, not a peep. But if I know Tommy I am pretty sure he will be on his best behaviour. He is not generally a fast mover in the love stakes!'

'Alex, listen I can't see you tonight. I am working,' she explained as she pulled a sad face.

Alexander feigned being shot in the heart, 'Argh, you have broken my heart' as he fell to the ground and then popped up. Alice laughed, his amateur dramatics group was already paying dividends.

'Sorry!'

'Not to worry, we have the rest of our lives,' he replied as he popped a kiss on her forehead.

This time it was her turn to act out her feelings, she put her fingers to her mouth and pretended to be sick but secretly she loved the way he seemed to be devoted to her.

****

Sarah found a shop that sold some trainers and swapped her heels for them, the pavements in Rome were so uneven and walking in heels was becoming hazardous and not to mention, painful. She was pleased that she had had the foresight to bring her skinny jeans with her and they looked nice with her crisp white tight fitting, bodice like shirt.

She had washed her hair and incredibly the combination of soft water and the excellent shampoo and conditioner in the hotel had left her hair full of volume and beautifully shiny. She decided to wear it down, long and flowing past her shoulders. The natural kinks in her hair meant her hair had perfect waves.

She noticed that she was attracting attention from the Italian men as they walked through the streets and whilst not deliberately courting it, it was really brightening her day.

Tommy was beginning to get a little annoyed by the attention Sarah was receiving, what was it with Italian men, couldn't they see that she was with him. He would have to walk alongside her and maybe hold her hand or drape his arm around her, then it would be clear this woman was not for the taking.

They reached the Spanish Steps and stood at the top taking in the City of Rome before them and then sat down for a breather. He put his arm around her and this time she let him. She couldn't help get absorbed by this city of romance.

They got up and holding hands ran down to the bottom

of the steps without stopping. Sarah was laughing all the way down that she forgot to breathe. When she finally did she laughed even more. She was laughing so hard she now found it hard to breathe and the more Tommy told her to calm down and breathe the funnier she found it and the worse she got. Tommy was starting to panic, at first he had found it funny but now she was struggling to breathe. Telling her to calm down just wasn't working so he tried saying nothing and then frantically started to look for a paper bag to see if that would help.. Just before he could find her one she miraculously stopped. The laughter disappeared just as abruptly as it had started.

'I am SOOOOOO sorry! I don't know what on earth was so funny but whatever it was, it was!'

'Jesus Sarah! You gave me such a fright, I thought I was going to lose you,' he sounded genuinely concerned.

'Really? Oh no don't worry, it happens every so often to me. A crazy five minutes of manic laughing and then it's all good.'

They stumbled upon the Trevi Fountain and it made Sarah stop in her tracks. It was bigger than she had imagined, the sound of the flowing water was soothing and the artistry just stunning.

'It is so beautiful!' She exclaimed. She wanted to stay here forever. Once again he put his arm around her and this time squeezed her tight.

'You are so special to me,' and he kissed her on her cheek.

Sarah felt all warm inside.

Just at that moment a street seller sidled up to them and thrust a huge red rose into their faces.

'For lady. Love.' his eager eyes impressed on them.

Tommy shooed him away 'No thank you.'

The man walked away annoyed. The Trevi Fountain was one of the most romantic destinations in the world and yet no one was buying his Roses. How could they say no to the most romantic flower on earth? He shook his head, he just didn't understand it.

'Legend has it that if you throw a coin into the Fountain you will return to Rome one day.'

'Oh yes I have heard that!'

'Yes it is true! If you throw two coins into it it will lead to a new romance and if you throw three into it it will lead to marriage.'

He reached into his pocket and pulled out three coins and handed them to Sarah. He turned her around so her back was facing towards the fountain and told her to throw the coins over her left shoulder.

She followed his instructions and heard a splash as each of the coins hit the water.

'Oh Tommy,' how had he had the coins ready in his pocket for this moment, had he planned it all along?

'Shhh,' he put his fingers on her lips, he pulled her closer to him and kissed her gently on the lips and then went back for a longer kiss. They both felt electricity shoot through their bodies and pulled away.

'I shouldn't, I really shouldn't.'

'Please Sarah, don't say anything. Enjoy this for what it is.' He held her hand and pulled her away from the crowds and they headed towards the shopping district. Sarah felt cold, her body was full of goosebumps. She felt shaken by this overtly romantic gesture.

Walking into the Gucci store Tommy pointed at a suit and then pointed to himself. What was he doing Sarah thought? The sales assistant however understood perfectly. In front of him was a scruffy man and a woman who clearly knew how to dress to show off her assets. He led the way to the back of the store, invited Sarah to sit down and made a sign to indicate that this could take a while as he put his hands together and made a sleeping gesture at her.

He then brought out numerous suits for Tommy to try. Sarah had never seen Tommy in a suit and now here she was sat watching him as he tried them on and asking for her opinion. He looked so good in the suits but as Sarah knew she was a sucker for a man in a suit she tried not to show that she was too keen for him to change his appearance. She did wonder what the reason was behind this sudden style transformation. That said Tommy looked equally comfortable in a suit as he did in his usual student style. He must have gone to a stuffy prep school where it was the norm to be all dressed up of course, so little wonder that was the case.

Tommy saw the gleam in Sarah's eyes the first time he walked out of the changing room in a tailored suit. He saw the way her pupils had enlarged and her eyes had widened with passion. This was the effect he had hoped it would elicit. A suit was definitely the way to go with her. He wished that the sales assistant hadn't brought out so many suits. He was finding it hard to choose which to buy, he asked Sarah for her opinion and she had just shrugged and said she didn't really know, she liked them all.

In the end he chose a dark blue, slim fitting suit and bought a white shirt to wear under it and a pair of shiny, lace up shoes.

He handed over his credit card and popped his student clothes into the Gucci paper bag.

'Very dapper!' Sarah held him close and felt that warmth

all over again.

'Sarah, I would love to buy you something too. Those trainers are indeed very lovely but this evening I would love to take you out for dinner. Please feel free to choose a pair of shoes for our evening together.'

Sarah was surprised. 'Really? Are you sure? We could head back to the hotel so I can change. It is no problem, honestly.'

He had been to Rome before and knew where there was a wonderful, smart and trendy restaurant close by. There was no point delaying the evening by returning to the hotel.

'Please choose something Sarah in here, it is my gift to you for planning my event. It will be my pleasure.'

She looked around the store and settled on a simple pair of Gucci leather heels. She tried them on and they fitted perfectly.

'You know it would be a shame to not buy a dress to go with them.'

'Oh no I really couldn't,' she protested but he insisted and walked over to a mannequin wearing a black long length slinky halterneck dress 'I was thinking something like this would be perfect, do you like it?'

Like it, she loved it. It was absolutely stunning, so simple and yet so elegant. He had such exquisite taste she was speechless but managed to mumble a faint 'yes, very much so'.

The sales assistant quick as a flash was standing beside her with an identical dress in his hands which he handed to her and this time it was her turn to disappear into the changing room.

It fitted her like a dream, skimming her body and enhancing the good points of her figure whilst managing to hide a multitude of sins. How could he possibly have just looked at the dress and known that it would suit her. It seemed that Tommy was full of hidden talents, perhaps now was the time to delve deeper and get to know this sexy, foppish aristocrat.

She pulled back the curtain and walked outside. Tommy took in a deep breath 'Amazing, just amazing. We shall have it, no need to wrap. The lady will be wearing it out.'

The sales assistant took payment and then removed the tags.

Tommy and Sarah dressed in top to toe Gucci looked every inch a powerful and glamourous couple.

They waltzed out the shop hand in hand and Tommy led her out into the darkness of Rome's cobbled streets.

Sarah wondered if they had to walk far because her killer heels were indeed killing her, except yet again she found herself saying what she was thinking out loud.

'No, not far at all, just a little way this way and a little over there and then we shall be there,' he reassured her.

They soon arrived at their destination, at least Sarah guessed this was where they were heading as the trendy beats were bellowing out into the deserted back street, the noise got louder and then bam she came face to face with it. Two floors of restaurant in a slick wall to ceiling windowed building. She could see right in and now she could understand why he had bought her the dress as well. Whilst the casual outfit she was wearing earlier was perfect for the day, the evening crowd in this joint were all uber stylish and impeccably dressed. The two of them certainly fitted right in.

She could barely hear what the waiter was saying but despite the place being crowded with wall to wall people a table for two was found and they sat down.

'How did you know about this place,' she yelled.

'Huh? Oh I have been here before with friends.'

'Oh! It is nice!'

'The food is fabulous.'

They both ordered bruschetta to start and then she ordered a carbonara and he a seafood spaghetti dish that was full of the heads of the crustaceans. He told her of how the first time he had ordered it he wasn't entirely sure which bits to eat and which bits to leave but now he was practically a Master Chef Professional. He asked her if she wanted to try some but she politely declined. She loved her food but mostly when it didn't look like the thing she was eating.

White wine and coffees were also on the agenda and she took care not to drink too much this time. The waiter came over with the dessert menu and they ordered Tiramisu which was just about the ideal way to end the meal. Smooth, creamy sweet mascarpone mixed with rich coffee soaked sponge was just the best Italian dessert she had ever tasted and felt utterly and delectably satiated in every sense.

In the warm candlelight Tommy's appeal was ever increasing and she wondered if it was the alcohol talking but let herself be led out into the cool streets and they started to walk towards a Metro stop arm in arm. He stopped her, leant against a wall and kissed her passionately this time. She felt powerless to resist, she had fallen well and truly in love with this city and Tommy. She could feel the sparks flying between them and she didn't want it to stop.

He pulled away just as she went back for more.

'We have to get going, we need to get the train and I don't expect you can run in those heels.'

He was right of course! Sarah nuzzled into his arms on the train as he placed a protective and supportive arm around her. She never wanted this romance to end.

They stood on the escalator, lovers in arms and let it take the strain. And then as they came up out of the station, Sarah saw something that made her stop in her tracks, rooted to the spot.

CHAPTER SIXTEEN

There staring down at her was a huge billboard with Adam posing in just his underwear. So he WAS a model. Her first instincts had been right, why hadn't he been able to tell her. It was a mighty fine body as well it might be for someone who models underwear. A smooth, gently ripped body with what was quite clearly a golden spray tan.

'What's the matter, you look like you have seen a ghost?'

'I, uh,I uh,' Sarah could barely get her words out. This was not at all what she had been expecting.

'Are you ok? Seriously I am worried about you, what with the earlier breathing issues. Do you have asthma?'

Sarah composed herself 'Sorry, I am fine. I thought I knew that guy but I guess he just looks familiar because I must have seen him advertising something or other in one of my magazines.'

Tommy wasn't convinced, that was quite some reaction to an advert.

Sarah felt all weird now, the romantic spell had been

broken and she just wanted to get back to her hotel room.

'Well goodnight Tommy. It has been nice,' she was cool towards him.

'Night Sarah,' he went to kiss her but she pulled away. What the hell was all that about? What a way to end an evening he thought.

Back in her room Sarah got out her phone and began writing a text to Adam. Seeing him almost naked had stirred something in her and she couldn't believe that she had allowed herself to fall for the charms of Tommy. She was completely confused.

Whatever she typed out wasn't coming out right so she typed and deleted her message a few times before settling on the following -

'Hey Adam, I kind of promised myself I would wait to contact you when I was back in the UK but well I had a few spare minutes so thought why not… oh btw what is it that you do again?'

She read it back to herself, when she had written it it had seemed perfect, now she wasn't so sure. It did seem a bit random and it was very late, he would probably think she was drunk. Then she hit on another idea - perhaps she should return to where the billboard was and take a photograph of it and then send that to him. That would let him know in no uncertain terms she knew exactly what he did for a living.

She deleted the text before she accidently sent it. This was stupid, she would talk to him when she got back but had second thoughts about the billboard and snuck out of the hotel to take a sneaky picture to keep on her phone without having Tommy stuck to her side.

****

Tommy lay in bed running through the events of the evening over and over in his head. He did feel sleepy but there was something really odd about Sarah's behaviour and he wanted to see if he could work out what it was. She was blowing hot and cold and whilst not the smartest brain on the block when it came to women he was totally flummoxed. Right up until the escalator they had been having a ball and then, yes that was it. It was the billboard, who was the mystery guy that had made Sarah change in an instant?

A text came through from Alex.

'Alice and I were wondering if you fancied meeting up in Paris. You and Sarah. Kind of like a double date ;-) Don't tell her though, Alice wants to surprise her!'

'I don't know if that is such a good idea to be honest Alex'

'Go on, it will be fun!'

'I don't know Alex, I don't think she is really the type of girl who would appreciate it'

It seemed rather childish to him and he wanted to be all sophisticated for her now....although if she was the type to fancy an underwear model there really wasn't much hope for him he thought.

'Too late. We have booked our tickets. See you soon!'

Oh shit, he really wasn't sure about this little turn of events. If they thought it was going to chivvy the romance along, after what had just happened, he wasn't at all convinced. Then again Alice knew Sarah better than anyone else right now so he would have to just trust her to know what she was doing in this department.

He heard a commotion outside his window and got out of bed, pulling back the heavy red velvet curtains to peer out, he saw two taxi drivers arguing over a customer at the hotel entrance. Just as he was about to turn away and return to bed he noticed from the corner of his eye a person that looked very much like Sarah. What was she doing outside at this time of night, he was sure it was her, he had drunk a bit at the restaurant but he was not drunk and it was most definitely not his mind playing tricks.

****

Sarah flopped down onto her bed and looked at the picture she had taken of Adam in his underwear. Caught on camera. Why hadn't he just said what he did for a living, she couldn't understand why he had lied to her, of course he hadn't actually lied, just been economical with the truth or actively avoided telling her anything. Mysterious Adam. Except now she knew exactly what he was, a David Gandy wannabe.

Sarah had thought dumping David and pushing him out of the picture would simplify things in her mind but seeing Adam today albeit not in the flesh had completely complicated things again. Her mind was as confused as ever. She wondered if she should do a Pros and Cons list with both Adam and Tommy, yes that could work and make things clearer for her to help her make her mind up.

Tommy was nice but perhaps she should come clean and tell him that she was sort of seeing someone else but then again they had only been on one official date, there wasn't any need to cut her options before she had had a chance to date them both. Americans did this all the time, kept their options open whilst they dated a few people to see who they wanted to go exclusive with. There was no difference here she reasoned. Tommy had been so exceptionally kind and romantic in Rome AND he was honest, which was a huge bonus as far as she was concerned, and yet she was being so dishonest and couldn't help but feel guilty. Before this Tempting Trio had surfaced she had been a strictly one man kind of woman. Oh she didn't know what to do but right now she should get some sleep, her eyelids were getting droopy and she was finding it hard to focus on anything.

Next morning she woke up to find she was still wearing the Gucci dress and had mascara smeared across her face, had she been crying in her sleep?

She joined Tommy for breakfast and sipped her latte slowly, savouring her warm, flaky pastries and being careful not to drop even one tiny little crumb.

Tommy wanted to ask her what was so important that it had made her leave the hotel last night but part of him wanted to keep quiet and wait to see if she would bring it up in general discussion. Needless to say Sarah didn't mention a thing to him which left him even more baffled. He was dying to know but he just couldn't bear to ask in case he didn't like the answer she gave him.

She glanced at her phone, she had missed a call from Alice, she must remember to take her phone off silent – also waiting to be read was a text from Alice.

'Sarah, what is going on with our Instagram, why have you uploaded a picture of man who looks suspiciously like Adam posing in his underwear on our company account?' Sarah could almost hear the angry tone in Alice's text.

Oh she hadn't, she couldn't have. She checked Instagram, she could have and she had. Worst of all it was going viral with thousands of likes and with people sharing the picture on Facebook and Twitter which let everyone know exactly where it was sourced from. She wanted to cry. She must have leant on her phone whilst sleeping and somehow managed to upload it. She didn't know what to do, if she removed it people may ask questions but if it remained up it bore absolutely no relevance to what Perfect Events did or the general impression it wanted to give.

She should call Alice right away. 'Will you excuse me Tommy, I have to make a business call. If you want to check out of the room and wait for me in reception the taxi will be here at 9.30am to pick us up.'

'No problem.'

It was only 8.30 so with an hour to go Tommy went up for some more food and coffee. He loved it when she came across all professional like that.

Come on, pick up Sarah willed Alice to answer the phone. She had had no luck calling Alice's mobile and was hoping that Alice was already in the office.

'Good morning Perfect Events.'

'Oh thank god! Alice it's me.'

'Sarah, did you get my message?'

'I did, I honestly don't know how that happened,' and she launched into a huge explanation.

'I was with Tommy all day, we had the most AMAZING day together in Rome seeing the sights and if I am entirely honest, please don't get angry Alice, I think I am falling in love with the client. I know, I know it is so unprofessional and I don't blame you if you sack me after the big event. Oh it was just so nice, we went to Gucci and he bought me an outfit for going out in, and when I say a new outfit I mean a dress and shoes to wear with it. We went to this incredible restaurant and ate delicious Italian food…' And on she went not forgetting to include every last detail.

Alice was getting impatient, she had work to do.

'Can you get to the point of how and why you uploaded THAT pic please Sarah?'

'And so we came out of the metro and there he was, my Adam staring right down at me as if to say that even though I wasn't in the same country as him he had his eye on me. I felt so bloody guilty for kissing Tommy, like a naughty school girl I had to abruptly stop things going any further with Tommy. When we got back to the hotel, I left Tommy in his room and went back to get a picture of the advert, why I have no idea. I then fell asleep on my bed. So you see it wasn't really my fault at all, it was just a horrible accident!'

'Right,' why did Sarah explain herself in a million words when a few would have done?

'So I am calling really to ask what I should do, shall I delete the picture or leave it up?'

'Honestly Sarah…I think it could do our company more damage and create more questions if we remove it. It does seem hugely popular and so far we haven't had any bad publicity so in a bizarre way you may have done Perfect Events a huge favour. All this free publicity and all that.'

'Ok, I am sorry Alice.'

'Sooooo a male model eh? Lucky girl!'

'Oh don't! It is ridiculous. I can't compete with those model girls that he meets every day.'

'You don't need to. He chased you remember! So what

are you going to do about Tommy?'

'I have no idea.'

'Yeah hard choice isn't it – on the one hand you could be dating Tommy a cute aristocrat and on the other hand you could be dating a hunky male model. Sure beats that married man you used to see… Oh by the way I had to block David's number from the work phone. He was being such a nuisance.'

'What??? Really? Oh and thanks for being absolutely no help in helping me choose.'

'Well let me know when you do!'

Alice shook her head, weren't they getting too old for all this drama, evidently not if Sarah's love life was any indication. She was so relieved she had found Alex and things had calmed down for her. She wasn't made to deal with drama in the same way that Sarah seemed to attract it.

Sarah sent a text to her sister 'Will be back from business trip Saturday, will pop home then. Love you x.'

Charlotte replied immediately 'OK see you then.'

Sarah checked out of her room and waited in the lobby for the taxi to arrive, there was no sign of Tommy, and considering he had had plenty of time to get ready she was surprised to not find him sat there already.

Tommy came running down the hall, just a day later and he was already back in his converse and skinny jeans she noted. She glanced at her watch, there was still plenty of time to check out, why on earth was he so flustered.

'You OK Tommy?'

'Yes, I went back to sleep and thought I had overslept, I

must get a watch.'

'Honestly, I have no idea how people can function without a watch, I can't live without mine. Sure a phone has the time on it but I don't always have my phone near me.'

'Alright Miss Perfect, we are not all like you.'

Sarah was about to respond with a witty comeback but decided against it. Not being sure what was up with him she didn't want to cause any friction before their next Castle viewing. Thankfully the taxi arrived and they hopped in. Leaving the busy centre of Rome was an ordeal in itself, Sarah stared out of the window at the traffic jam with cars going absolutely nowhere. She was beginning to fret that they would be late for their appointment and couldn't help but keep looking at her watch. A policeman was stood in the middle of the road blowing his whistle and directing traffic, it was still chaotic though.

She spotted two car crashes and let out a scream when it looked as if they were about to have a head on crash themselves. The taxi driver looked in his rear-view mirror and smiled at her.

'It's OK huh, this is Rome,' he shrugged his shoulders and she got the feeling that this kind of thing happened all the time over here. It wasn't great for her nerves though, her stomach was tensing up.

Tommy squeezed her hand 'You OK, it's a bit nail biting isn't it?'

She was grateful for the simple gesture. Soon they had made their way out of the city centre and were cruising at a nice pace through the countryside. Italy was such a lovely place, she wondered if the Castle would live up to their expectations.

'I spy with my little eye something beginning with C.'

Sarah laughed 'A castle?'

And there it was. Smaller than the one in Germany but with more external charm. She asked the driver to wait for them and knocked on the thick wooden door. She listened as it seemed to echo throughout the whole building but in reality was probably just the hallway.

This time a man opened the door.

'Benvenuti Mr and Mrs Fawsett.'

He thought they were married, she had to correct him before they went any further.

'Ciao,' she thought she would try and impress him before telling him that they were not married.

'We, I mean I am not married to Mr Fawsett, I am Sarah Dawes from Perfect Events, we spoke on the phone,' she hoped he remembered her.

'Ah si! Miss Dawes, A pleasure to meet you,' he took her hand in his own soft ones and greeted her warmly.

'I am sorry we are a little late, I misjudged the Rome traffic.'

'No problemo, it is fine. The traffic is always bad. We are used to it,' Sarah sighed he was so nice and warm and friendly and forgiving.

'Please come this way.'

The castle was a lot more homely than the one in Germany. Where that had been huge and imposing it was in essence a shell that could be dressed up. This one had obviously been under a complete internal décor transformation. No detail had been spared to take it back to its era and it looked like no expense had been spared either. The bathroom was lavish and luxurious with marble tiling and lots of gilt edging and extravagant decorative taps. It even had a huge feature bath in the corner. She would love to take a bath in that. Tommy looked over at Sarah, by the look on her face he was sure they had the same thoughts – THAT BATH, they needed to try it out and it was big enough for two. He caught her eye and grinned at her. She had to look away before she burst into a fit of giggles. Naughty thoughts were obviously being shared by them both.

Giovanni led the way to the catering kitchen, it was a huge space and the stainless steel design ultra-modern with every kitchen mod con that you would ever need, ideal for the caterers she thought. This was looking very, very good.

They moved into the Great Hall and took a sharp intake of breath. It was absolutely stunning, the whole theme was carried throughout the castle. This castle was fit for Hollywood royalty, in fact Sarah recalled when she was searching on the internet that top Hollywood stars had stayed and partied here. She wasn't sure their budget would stretch to the hiring of the bedrooms, actually she was certain it wouldn't but the party rooms were beyond fabulous and would need little or no work to bring them up to scratch.

They walked outside to perfectly manicured lawns and sweet low hedges. Lights across the gardens gave a beautiful glow to the fading light and lit up the pathways and soon the whole building was lit up as darkness fell.

'So if the weather is supposed to be good we can have tables made up outside too, there is plenty of room for guests to move around.'

It was very pretty outside and there was no issue with noise from the band or DJ affecting any neighbours, they were miles from anywhere! She liked the idea of outside partying too but had to work out the logistics of it all. Would it dilute things in the Great Hall if everyone was outside? It all seemed pretty perfect but she bore in mind that there was still one more venue to view. This place however was the frontrunner she was clear on that.

'Thank you so much Giovanni, it is a fabulous place you have here. We shall be in contact next week with our decision.'

'For sure, it is very popular with all who come,' he beamed.

'We shan't take up anymore of your time, thank you once again.'

'Oh Sarah, I have something for you,' he said in his smooth Italian accent and he handed her a little box.

'Oh thank you!' She didn't know what it contained yet but would unwrap it once back in the taxi.

'Please, open it,' he stood there waiting expectantly. She had no choice but to open it in front of him.

'Oh, OK,' she unwrapped it and saw a box of 'Baci' in silver and blue packaging, it was chocolate.

'Baci means kisses,' he explained. 'It is a traditional gift that all Italians give. Enjoy.'

He kissed her on both cheeks and did the same to Tommy and bid them both goodbye.

She had no idea if it was true or not but she was going to look forward to eating them in the taxi to the airport.

'I loved that castle!' they said in unison.

Sarah reminded Tommy not to make up his mind just yet, there was one more place to see. Truth be known though she wished she could stop the search right there and then. Part of her wanted to call up the Paris Castle and cancel their appointment but time wasting wouldn't be good for 'Perfect Events' reputation and it would mean that they would need to cancel flights and accommodation that had already been booked and paid for. No, they had to continue with their journey.

This time it didn't take long at all to get back to the airport. The traffic had disappeared into the Rome night. They found a coffee shop and sat down. Sarah started updating her spreadsheet and Tommy popped in his ear phones and began rocking in tempo. The tinny sound coming from his ears was making it hard to concentrate so she made a dramatic gesture and raised her hands in despair.

'How can I possibly work with that racket?'

'Sorry! I can turn it down.'

'I would be most grateful.'

There was that strong character of Sarah's that Tommy liked so much, he wondered if he annoyed her on purpose to elicit that kind of response and decided he wasn't that clever.

'Someone's got an admirer,' he teased.

'What?' Who?' She seemed keener than Tommy liked.

He had started this so he had to finish it.

'Giovanni, he gave you Baci. It's like a Rolo – you only give it to someone you love.'

'Oh don't be silly! He just wants our business, he was buttering me up. You could call it bribing me, Frau Jung did the same with the tea and biscuits remember?'

'Sarah I really do like you, you know.'

Where did that come from? Sarah wanted to avoid any more romance, from now on, on this trip she was going to be in work mode, this was no way to carry on with a client and her head was so messed up with emotions she was finding it hard to concentrate.

'Tommy, I am going to say this only once so please listen carefully. I am quite ashamed of my behaviour in Rome. I took my eye off of the ball and lost the purpose of our trip. You are my client, I have a job to do. I like you too. You know that, I know you do but for now I need to focus on the task in hand. Once the job is done and if we still feel the same way when we are back in London then we can take a look at giving dating a go but not before.'

Wow, she had no idea where that had come from, it was quite the little speech. She sort of meant it and was trying to convince herself too. They were heading to Paris, yet another romantic city and she knew if she hadn't said anything Tommy would probably have continued his not so unwelcome charm offensive. She wasn't sure what she wanted anymore and she wanted to have a clear head. A break from romantic gestures may just give her the space she needed.

She was clearly quite serious about this thought Tommy, she looks so stern and her voice didn't waiver once. So matter of fact, if she had thought this was going to put him off it hadn't, if anything it had made his resolve even stronger. This woman was formidable and knew exactly what she wanted in life. He would respect her decision but he wasn't going to let her off that easily when they were back in London. This was THE woman for him.

Flying into Charles De Gaulle Airport Sarah had a good view of Paris lit up at night through the airplane window. It was so pretty she wished she had booked to stay longer once the actual business trip was over but she didn't fancy being alone in a romantic city so she hadn't and she knew that she really should get home and see her family as she had promised. Alice would love this, she was certain Alice had never been to Paris, she preferred far flung exotic holidays with guaranteed sun than city breaks, whereas Sarah was happy taking in the sights of a city.

'Wheee, we are landing,' the sound came from Tommy. Back to immature Tommy. Actually it suited him more than grown up Tommy she thought. She didn't really want to change who he was, that wouldn't be fair, particularly as she had no intention of changing herself. She wanted someone to love her for who she was so what was she thinking by trying to change the whole essence of Tommy. Then she remembered that actually she hadn't made Tommy change at all, she hadn't said a word. He had done it all for her entirely off his own back. Such a romantic thing to do. It must be true he did like her.

It was a bit of a bumpy landing, so much so that it had been a bit touch and go for a minute. Once they had landed the whole airplane burst into applause relieved that they had touched down safely. It didn't stop a woman in front of Sarah sobbing loudly whilst being comforted by the passenger next to her. Tommy sniggered, rather inappropriately she thought.

Suddenly Sarah felt homesick, this whistle-stop work trip was clearly troubling her. She had over indulged in rich food and the lack of sleep was taking its toll. She just wanted to return to normality, travel always sounded so glamourous but the reality couldn't be further from the truth. She was literally aching for her bed, she hadn't got along with a single pillow in the rooms that she had stayed in and now her neck was hurting. She yearned for a simple breakfast of Porridge and Ryvita lunches. Still just one more day or so and she would finally be home.

She hadn't forgot about Adam, she had looked at his picture as often as she could. She needed to speak to him.

CHAPTER SEVENTEEN

Paris was warm this evening and was set to be the same again tomorrow. She already liked the place, there was nothing worse than arriving at a destination to find it pouring with rain. Having just eaten on the plane all Sarah wanted to do was get to the hotel and sleep. Tomorrow they were planning on an early start and she wanted to be on top form. Tommy offered to walk her to her room but she politely declined.

The hotel was one that an estate agent would call 'Bijou', it certainly was small. The toilet was in a cupboard whilst the hand basin was on the other side of the room in another cupboard sized room.

It was very basic with no frills but this was not a problem, it literally was intended as a bed for the night and no soon as her head had hit the pillow Sarah had drifted off to asleep.

Tommy was texting Alex.

'Any budding romance has been nipped in the bud. She has categorically stated no hanky panky in Paris, you still want to come tomorrow?'

'It's all booked, no point cancelling. Alice is looking forward to it actually and don't spill a bean to Sarah but I am going to propose!'

'What??'

'Isn't it too soon? I mean you hardly know her!'

'No way. Never too soon Tommy boy! When you know you know, she is the best thing that has ever happened to me. I am not letting her slip through my fingers,' Tommy started nodding his head, it was true when you knew, you just knew, he couldn't deny it.

Breakfast consisted of chocolate chaud (hot chocolate) and warm croissants which they dipped into the chocolate drink.

Sarah spoke first 'So plans for the day – see the Chateau this morning and then I was thinking we should head back into Paris for some touristy sight-seeing things and dinner. Fly back to London first thing tomorrow.'

'Yuh, absolutely,' he didn't want to sound overly keen now but trying to maintain a median that wasn't overly keen and not completely disinterested was proving a little hard.

Last night he had gone back out and bought a bottle of red wine which he had drunk all by himself, he had then called Arabella and tried to engage in some sexy chat with her which she had responded with by laughing down the phone at him.

'Are you drunk Tommy Fawsett? Get back to London pronto so I can see that cheeky little face of yours. We have a LOT of catching up to do!'

'Um yah, see you Sat night for the bash, Ciao mwah,' he

breathed a little too heavily at the thought of seeing the sexy Lady Arabella again.

He needed some affection badly, if Sarah wasn't going to give him any he had no other choice.

And then he had remembered how he knew Arabella, they had once, briefly, shared a nanny. Had it come back to her too?

'Tommy, are you being distant because I have rebuffed your advances? I said we would see what happened when we got back to London.'

'Me! Distant? Honestly Sarah you blow hotter than the Sahara and colder than the Artic. I just think you are playing games with me and my poor heart.'

He squeezed her arm. 'Just kidding! Come on we have a Chateau to see.'

The French countryside was a lot more rustic than the Italian one and it seemed like they were heading far into the hills, Sarah made a note of the time taken to reach here from the centre of Paris. There literally was nothing else around here, it was remote and wild and then there it stood. A fabulously regal Chateau with a moat! A moat and a drawbridge! And proper turrets and towers. Oh this was pretty magnificent. This beat the other two hands down when it came to entrances, she imagined guests being brought in by horse and carriages. The carriages would be black and the horses too. Her imagination was running away with her and she was letting it do so.

'Wow!'

'I was thinking the same! Let's see what inside holds.'

Monsieur Chevalier was ready and waiting for their

arrival, he must have seen them arrive as he opened the door just as they were about to knock. Chevalier, the irony was not lost on Sarah. She whispered to Tommy.

'His name is Monsieur Chevalier, it means knight and is from Cheval, French for Horse, a bit appropriate don't you think?'

Tommy nodded and just as he was about to reply the 6ft 3 Monsieur Chevalier was looming down on them, he found him slightly intimidating.

'Bonjour Mademoiselle Dawes, Monsieur Fawsett. It is my pleasure to show you around our grand Chateau. Perhaps a warm drink before we start?'

'That would be lovely.'

'I shall take the opportunity to show you around the kitchens at the same time, we have two.'

The chateau was imposing and a little eerie, the doors and floorboards creaked and even though it was still the morning Sarah had the feeling that at the very next corner she would come face to face with a ghost. Of course it didn't happen but when she found herself staring at a knight's armoured statue she did take a closer look just to check that no one was lurking inside it. Now she knew how Scooby Do and Shaggy felt. This place felt haunted and she didn't fancy returning after dark.

She felt a hand on her shoulder, it made her jump and scream out loud.

'Ahhhhh,' she listened as it echoed around the empty walls.

'Hey, it's only me!' he said in a kindly voice.

'Tommy, why would you do that?' She jabbed him in the

stomach.

'You seem freaked out, perhaps this place isn't for us?'

'I don't know what it is about it but this place just gives me the creeps and I have goosebumps all along my arm and not in a good way,' she held out her arm so he could see them.

'But, Tommy this is your event and if you like it then we will go with it, I totally respect your decision,' she hoped beyond hope he didn't want to though.

'No, I mean I think this place is pretty awesome obviously but it is probably too large for our requirements.'

'Where has Monsieur Chevalier disappeared to?' Sarah shivered, it was warm outside but inside it was decidedly chilly.

'Ooh I don't know! He was just behind me.'

'Can we get out of here please?'

'Ha ha Sarah, you really are scared here aren't you?'

She punched him in the arm.

'It's not funny!'

He rubbed his arm 'Ow that hurt! OK, OK.'

Just at that moment Monsieur Chevalier popped his head out of a doorway 'Would you like to take a look at one of our towers, the sights are something quite special?'

'Actually Monsieur Chevalier I afraid we cannot stay any longer, unfortunately we have another appointment to get to and our Taxi is waiting outside,' she was eager to leave and made a mental note to not even bother adding this Chateau to her spreadsheet.

'Bye!' Tommy said cheerily as they sped away and they just heard the words 'Au Revoir' floating in the wind as Monsieur Chevalier replied.

'Not if I can help it,' muttered Sarah under her breath.

Sarah cuddled up close to Tommy and he moved in closer too and wrapped his arms around her. He tilted her face up and looked into her eyes.

'Perhaps we should have gone with our instincts after all and cancelled that last appointment to spend the whole day in Paris instead!'

How did he know that that is what she had been thinking of doing, she hadn't told him? Perhaps he knew her better than she thought or perhaps he had magical mind reading powers.

'Have you ever done magic Tommy?'

'Huh, no why do ask?'

'Oh no reason.'

She stayed in his safe arms until they arrived into the outskirts of Paris where they ditched the taxi and hopped onto the Metro to make their way into the centre. They had figured quite correctly that it would be jammed with city traffic and this would maximise the time they had left.

Just then Sarah received a text from Adam.

'Not long now... x'

She smiled at her phone, Adam was going to have to wait, she had family matters to attend to and then she would confront this red hot underwear model with what she had seen in Rome.

Adam's phone was going crazy, ever since that picture had gone viral he was fast becoming one of the most sought after male models in the industry. Rather than having to chase jobs he was being chased for jobs and managers were falling over themselves to take over his management. He was being wined and dined almost daily by industry bigwigs and looking at just this month's workload he realised he could finally give up the day job in boring but pays well recruitment. It was all down to that Instagram share from 'Perfect Events' so in a way Sarah inadvertently had had a huge influence on his career without her even seemingly knowing. Strangely she hadn't mentioned a thing to him and he wanted to thank her personally for this amazing turn of events.

His work phone rang 'Adam, where have you been? I have been trying to get you all morning! Why aren't you answering your phone? Am I not still your manager?' She fired off the questions.

Adam sighed, Katie.

'Katie, I had to turn my phone off as it just doesn't stop ringing. The guys in the office are pretty pissed off to be honest and I think I am about to lose my job.'

'No need to worry about that, let them sack you. You are going to be a multimillionaire, I can guarantee it. The TV stations all want to interview you. This is a superb human interest story - you know – Man becomes internet sensation through one photo. Anyway I am in talks with them and interviews will be held soon, you will say yes won't you? I reckon we could do a couple and get top whack for them rather than have you appearing everywhere but we shall see what the offers are first.' And on and on Katie went – 'let's do this, let's do that' that very soon Adam was tuning out and picturing himself saturating the world's media.

Adam the social media star model – he liked that.

'Adam, Adam?'

'Yes, sorry phone cut out.'

'Adam, don't pull that line with me, this is your work phone, you weren't listening were you?' She demanded. 'I am not doing this for my benefit you know, this is your career and if you don't want to put the effort in, I sure as hell won't be.'

'I was saying that I think we should speak to 'Perfect Events' and get their side of the story. Perhaps organise some joint interviews.'

'Really? I am not so sure,' he thought about it, joint interviews would mean spending more time with the delectable Sarah. Yes, he would love to know what it was exactly that had prompted Sarah to share his photo on the work account which in turn had helped snowball his modelling career. Hurry up Sarah and come home.

'Oh there is just one other thing…I need you in Paris this evening. Apparently you are going to be doing a party wear shoot for Marks and Spencer, they want you to replace David Gandy in their Tops and Tails range. The shoot will be at the Eiffel Tower, can you do it? They said it was a test shoot but I am not convinced anyone would fly someone out on location for just a test shoot.'

'Sure, can you arrange travel for me? I will leave the office pronto.'

'Perfect, the shoot will be around midnight so plenty of time to get there. By the sounds of it it sounds really romantic if you ask me. I am jealous, I wish I could accompany you!' Katie was wistful and wished she hadn't made plans to celebrate her wedding anniversary this evening so she could accompany her new star client.

Adam put the phone down and started to wind down his office work for the day. In a few hours he would be in Paris. Life was changing so fast for him and he was liking it a lot.

****

Sarah and Tommy had got hopelessly lost on the complicated Paris Metro, he had insisted it was one way, she had insisted it was the other. He won out and of course it was the wrong way and they had to spend precious time going back on themselves. She was seething inside and wondered why on earth he wouldn't just listen to her. She never said things unless she was totally confident she was right. Why did he have to be so bloody minded that his way was the only way. They sat in silence on the return journey, her with her arms folded and a face like she was sucking lemons, he as usual had popped his music on and was staring at the ceiling. They got off the train from separate doors and refused to acknowledge each other, she walking to the exit with purposeful strides and he dawdling behind in case he found himself directly behind her.

He broke the standoff first by calling out to Sarah 'Sarah, this is silly. Look I am sorry, I should have listened to you. You were right, we should have gone the way you wanted to go.'

She carried on walking 'I am not interested.'

'Oh come on, I said I was sorry. How long are you

going to keep this up for? We only have one day in Paris, don't spoil it.'

'I don't care to be honest. I have had enough of your childish behaviour.'

'Me! You have got to be joking. You need to grow up and figure out exactly what it is that YOU want!'

She was outraged 'How dare you talk to me like that, you know something, stuff Paris, I might just head to the airport right now,' she marched off in the opposite direction with absolutely no idea where she was heading.

Tears were falling down her cheeks, I guess this was what you would call a fiery relationship. They seemed to row a little too often for her liking. The fact was that she did care, she cared very much for what he thought and he thought she had to grow up.

He was right, she did have to make a decision. She wasn't cut out for this multi relationship juggling but was this an insight into what their relationship was going to be like if she did solely date him. She had read somewhere in Cosmo once that holidays put a lot of strain on relationships and that there was a high incidence of break ups on and when people returned from holiday. She had one thing in her favour regarding this, they were not actually dating.

Tommy ran after her and jumped in front of her to block her path, he couldn't let her leave. There was the surprise to come this evening. How could he make her stay, he had to think fast.

'Hey,' he wiped a tear from her face and hugged her, she didn't reciprocate as she wasn't quite ready to forgive him.

'Let's go on a Bus Tour this afternoon, it is the best way

to see all the sights don't you think? But first how about we get a bite to eat, I don't know about you but I am starving, hmmm?' he pleaded.

She softened her gaze and he knew that she was receptive to this gesture.

He steered her towards a traditional style café and they sat outside watching the traffic go by. They ordered two delightfully French Croque-Monsieurs – a ham and cheese toasted sandwich and 2 cokes. Tommy also ordered a beer. He felt like he deserved it.

The food must have been just what Sarah needed, she felt much better now and stared at the pretty cakes in the window and ordered a fresh cream éclair, she clearly needed a sugar fix. Tommy joined her and ordered an éclair too and then ordered two café au laits to go with them. French Café Culture was simply the best, it was laidback (the waitress had long disappeared) and being sat on a table on the pavement they were soaking up the atmosphere and being drenched in warm sunshine.

Tommy started fidgeting and looking around, where was the waitress, he needed to pay and go. The bus tour left at 2pm and he didn't want to miss it.

'Have you seen our waitress?'

'No, should we go in and get her?'

'No I don't think so, I think I can spot her over there, I can speak a bit of French I will call her.'

'Garcon!'

'Tommy, you just called our waitress a boy!'

'Oh heck did I? I thought that was how you called for the bill,' the waitress appeared not looking best pleased and then Tommy spoke once more.

'L'addition s'il vous plait,' she nodded and disappeared back into the café. She reappeared and slapped down the bill on the table and Sarah giggled. He had really pissed off the waitress. So he didn't just save it just for her she thought.

Tommy settled the bill even though Sarah had offered to do it and they found the stop where the Bus Tour started.

Picking up their headphones they made their way up to the top deck of the open top tour bus and headed straight for the back seats, this felt like a school trip and they were the naughty teenagers who had inevitably managed to give their teacher the slip. They selected the channel for English as their preferred language and off the bus went.

They stopped off at the Champs Elysees and walked down the famous road and did a bit of window shopping in the designer stores. They hopped back on and headed for the L'Arc de Triumphe and wandered up to the top to look out across the city. Then off they went to Notre Dame for a look around the grand cathedral and then finally to the Louvre, the queue was huge so they forgot about any ideas they had of going inside and seeing the world famous paintings, instead they had to settle for taking a few pictures of the triangular entrance outside.

Sarah was careful to remember to upload her Paris pictures onto Instagram, even the creepy Chateau and their delicious café lunch. For some reason people loved pictures of food so she was happy to oblige.

They then headed to The Eiffel Tower and although there was a queue it was moving fast, as befitting a capital city it wasn't complete without tat sellers, these ones were offering to write your name in wire, selling sticky men toys that you threw onto a wall and watched them climb down and the obligatory Rose sellers, this was Paris after all! A man walked up to them and tried to sell them bottles of water which they politely declined and then they made their way up to the top of the Tower. They stood there admiring the views across the city.

'It's breath-taking isn't it?'

'No, I think you will find that it's the atmospheric change that is doing that to you.'

Sarah dug her elbow into his ribs 'Will you be serious for one minute!'

'No you are right, it is. Paris is such a beautiful city. Even more so from way up high,' he agreed.

'It is a shame we won't get to see The Eiffel Tower at night, I bet it looks amazing.'

'Who says we can't, we have some spare time after dinner. Let's do it!'

They found a small café and topped up on sustenance, more coffee and pastries of course!

They hopped back on the Tour Bus and hopped off once the bus had arrived in the artistic district of Montmarte where they soaked up the creative atmosphere and even gave in to an offer for a caricature picture of the two of them and noticed that the artist had drawn a huge heart between them.

'This is brilliant, I am going to frame it and put it on my wall,' Tommy said.

'It is rather good! I thought he was going to draw a horrid jokey picture but actually he has captured our faces really rather well!'

They wandered up the hill to the Sacre Coeur Church and wandered around inside taking time to visit the Crypt. They stood and stared at the Apse Mosaic.

'Wow, this is quite heavenly don't you think? I love mosaics and as mosaics go this is exceptional.'

Tommy read the leaflet that they were handed at the entrance 'The mosaic is one of the largest in the world, it represents the risen Christ, clothed in white and with arms extended, revealing a golden heart. Surrounding him, in various sizes, a world of adorers is represented, including the Saints who protect France: the Virgin Mary and Saint Michael, Saint Joan of Arc, as well as a personification of France offering her crown and Pope Leo XIII offering the world.'

'Incredible, I have goosebumps. I am not remotely religious but I cannot help be moved by this.'

They then made their way up to The Dome by climbing up the 300 steep steps.

'More amazing views Tommy. I had no idea Paris was just so pretty.'

It was almost a shame that the party wouldn't be taking place in France but Sarah had already mentally planned to return, perhaps next time with her chosen boyfriend.

'Now this IS making me breathless,' Tommy was panting heavily.

'Someone is unfit! Not used to the exercise eh? Must be what happens when you are taken around everywhere by chauffeur driven car huh?'

'If you believe that... it is utter nonsense!'

'Don't worry, it is much easier getting back down again,' she reassured him. She didn't want to admit that her legs had turned to jelly and her knees were aching and would only get worse going back down the stairs. They had never been the same since she had dislocated them whilst falling trying to climb across some monkey bars when she was eighteen.

She held onto the rail and walked slowly behind him, she had watched as he had enthusiastically skipped his way down.

'Come on slow coach!' he yelled from down below.

'I am coming! Hold on,' she was irritated, Tommy had no patience or sympathy for others. She watched as an elderly man passed her on the stairs in a spritely manner.

Finally she reached the last step, ouch her knees were so sore now. At least on flat ground she could regain her composure and walk properly once again.

'My god you were like an old woman coming down those stairs.'

'Yes OK, don't rub it in!'

Tommy's phone beeped. A text from Alex.

'All set for this evening?'

'Yup. We will be there for 7pm.'

By now the sun was setting and so they headed to some souvenir shops. Sarah picked up a fridge magnet as she had done so in each of the cities they had visited. Ever since she was quite young she had bought a fridge magnet from wherever she had been. It was the only thing she had collected in her life and now her huge fridge was covered in all different shapes and sizes and types of fridge magnet.

She also picked up a few items for her family as gifts for when she went back home.

Tommy stared at them but didn't pick up anything although he was rather fond of a pen that had a floating dancing girl who lost her bikini when you started to write and a fridge magnet of a bottom wearing French knickers.

Sarah looked at him staring at the items.

'Shall I buy that for you?'

'Hmm? No! I think I will leave them.'

'Are you sure, I don't mind,' she really wanted him to feel ashamed at what had caught his attention but he seemed nonplussed.

Tommy knew a few of his friends would appreciate these joke items as gifts but thought better of putting his hand in his pocket and purchasing them in front of the lovely Sarah. From the look on her face he could see she was not impressed and wondered how the planned evening of Cabaret at The Moulin Rouge was going to go down.

'It's our last night Tommy.'

'Mmm, I know you are probably thinking never again but I have to say I have really enjoyed myself.'

'You would,' Sarah thought, she had had to do all the organising and making sure he was up and ready in time for each day's events but before she decided to write him off she remembered that as the Events Organiser that was actually her role. He was the client.

'Mmm,' she agreed. 'It has been fun and certainly interesting. There is never a dull moment with you Tommy Fawsett that is for sure!'

'Dinner Madam?' He said in his poshest Tommy accent which she had to admit made her legs wobble quite a bit.

'Why I would be delighted Sir Fawsett,' she attempted to reply in her poshest Sarah accent.

They both giggled and like a true gentleman he held out his arm for her to take and off they walked up the road.

They stopped at a delightful looking traditional French Brasserie, she peered in through the window and saw the dark wood and warm, cosy lighting and wished they were going to be eating in there.

'This looks nice don't you think Tommy?'

'Yes it does indeed,' as it happened this is where they were going to be having dinner. He wished he could have taken the credit for choosing this restaurant but Alex and Alice had found it earlier when they were sightseeing and booked the table for the four of them.

He pushed open the door and they walked inside.

It smelt fantastic and by now Sarah was starving. Tommy led the way to a booth and at that moment Alex and Alice stood up.

'SURPRISE!' they both shouted, their faces beaming.

'Oh my goodness! What are you doing here Alice! And WHO is this!?' Sarah was shocked, she had not been expecting this at all.

'I hope you don't mind us joining you, this is a business trip after all,' Alice winked at Sarah.

'Let me introduce you to Alexander …. He is a friend of Tommy's and also happens to be the new boyfriend that I was telling you about.'

Alex prodded her with genuine affection 'Hey you, not so much of the new please.'

'A pleasure to meet you Sarah, Alice has told me so much about you, as has Tommy I should say.'

'All good things I hope?' Sarah was feeling a bit put out and left footed. This was all a bit too cosy for her liking. They all knew each other, had they been talking about her behind her back? She hated the thought of that. A little niggling feeling in the back of her mind felt that this was more than just a chance meeting.

'Of course,' Tommy replied and she felt his arm around her and this time there was nowhere for her to escape…Here we go again so much for time to clear her head.

Still she had to make the most of it, a free dinner in a great restaurant in Paris with her best friend.

They all ordered the French Onion Soup to start which came with a big hulk of bread and a thick cheese covering that needed to be penetrated to reach the rich, dark and silky flavoursome soup below.

Naturally the only drink to accompany their meal was copious amounts of red wine. For their mains they all ordered Steak et Frites, Bien Sur. As you do. When in France, it is the only choice.

They all felt pretty stuffed after all that rich food but that pudding belly was calling Sarah and she convinced the others to join her in having a dessert.

For Sarah the obvious choice was a Crème Brulee that had been tempting her from the start and she wasn't disappointed. She tapped her spoon gently on the hard, crispy sugar coating to no avail, she then swapped to forcefully poking the sugar eventually cracking the topping so she could enjoy the soft vanilla crème underneath. She noticed Tommy looking at her from the corner of his eye so she seductively and playfully slurped the custard like consistency off of her spoon.

She is such a tease thought Tommy trying to ignore the stirrings in his trousers. Right now he was more than a little jealous of his friend Alex who was kissing Alice rather too passionately before his very eyes.

Sarah was also a little jealous of Alice and her new found happiness but was happy for her friend. She just wished that some of her romantic luck would rub off onto her. It was true that she had men falling at her feet but something wasn't clicking with any of them at this moment in time. She hardened her resolve to just focus on her career for the time being and see where life took her. It had worked for Alice so there was no reason it couldn't work for her.

She spied Tommy looking at her again but she refused to return his gaze. She could feel the wine going to her head and knew that with his winning smile she probably would be tempted to take things further tonight.

Alice managed to drag herself away from Alex's lips long enough to order a bottle of Champagne from the waiter which once they each had a glass in their hand made a toast to Tommy's party of the year. They joyfully downed it whilst gaining a few stares from the other diners who were looking at the jolly British party.

Sarah yawned and glanced at her watch, it was only 9.30pm but she was feeling sleepy. It was most probably the combination of rich food and alcohol and the brilliant warmth of the restaurant.

'Well, I best get back to the hotel, sorry for being such a

lightweight guys,' she declared.

'Oh no you don't' Alice grabbed her arm as she stood up to leave. We have one more surprise in store.

Alex gave Tommy a knowing look.

'What is it?' Sarah was struggling to stay awake.

Alice settled the bill and they walked off in the direction of the seedy streets of the Pigalle District. The cool air had soon sobered Sarah up and Tommy was holding onto her tightly. She noticed how there seemed to be scantily clad women on the streets trying to draw the men into various dubious establishments, they even tried to drag in Tommy and Alex disregarding or oblivious to the fact that they had women with them. Stopping abruptly Sarah looked up, they had arrived at the famous Paris Windmill.

The Moulin Rouge.

'You have got to be joking, I am not going in there. If you want to see topless women, go right ahead but count me out,' she was disgusted.

'Aw come on Sarah, it's just a bit of harmless fun. You can't go to Paris and not see the Cancan,' pleaded Alice.

'Not my idea of fun Alice. Sorry.'

Tommy took her in his arms. 'Sarah don't spoil this evening,' he brushed a strand of hair away from her face. 'Your best friend planned this as a surprise for us both, don't be a gooseberry.'

He really wanted to see the world famous Topless Cancan but knew if she didn't want to go he would feel obliged to accompany her back to the hotel which would mean missing out on the show.

'I really don't want to Tommy, honestly it's not my thing.'

'Please,' his eyes pleaded with her.

She looked over at Alice whose face was looking rather sad as she was being comforted by Alex.

She felt bad, it was true her good friend and business partner had come over to France to surprise her and she was acting like a spoilt brat. For the sake of keeping the peace she decided to relent.

'Oh OK then. I'll do it.'

'Good girl,' Tommy squeezed her arm 'We all appreciate it,' no one more so than him.

In an effort to join in and try to enjoy the cabaret show she ordered more alcohol. Once settled into their seats the show began and reluctantly Sarah had to admit it was actually rather better than she had been expecting, not great but not that bad. Yes there was nudity but she managed to ignore it whilst focusing on the dancer's incredibly long, lean legs and tapping her legs to the music.

Tommy spent the entire time with his eyes transfixed to the stage. It was evident that there had been a distinct lack of female presence in his adolescence and this was fuelling his desire and need for a woman.

Alice and Alex watched the show entwined in each other's arms, kissing and canoodling and every so often glancing in the direction of the stage when there was applause around them but they probably wouldn't be able to recount what they had seen if asked.

They left a little more drunk than when they had entered and started walking down the street in the direction of The

Eiffel Tower.

****

Adam had had to rush to make his Eurostar train and even then had only just made it in time, he settled down in his seat ready to have a snooze. He became aware of a girl sat opposite who hadn't taken her eyes off of him since the train had started to move. He half opened his eyes and she smiled at him.

'It's Adam isn't it?' She enquired.

'Er it depends who is asking,' he chuckled back at her.

She looked embarrassed and so he opened his eyes fully and gave her a look that said 'I am sorry.'

'Sorry to bother you but I just thought you looked familiar and then I remembered where I have seen you before, it's THAT underwear advert isn't it. Do you mind if we have a selfie together? My friends will be SO jealous that I am sat on the same train as you.'

Adam figured that as you just never knew how long your fame would last that he would embrace his fans and enjoy every second of it whilst he could. She couldn't have been more than sixteen and the thought did enter his head that it could potentially be contentious but he soon dismissed the thought and happily obliged by posing for a selfie with the girl.

'Thank you so much. You won't regret this.'

Was this a forewarning that he would? He very much hoped not. As it turned out the sixteen year old girl was the daughter of the head of International Marketing at a huge and iconic British Luxury Brand and little did he know that

that evening she would be going home to excitedly tell her mum what a lovely guy he was and why he simply had to head their New Year Campaign.

At Gare De Nord a taxi was waiting to whisk him off to The Eiffel Tower where the stylist and makeup artist were keenly awaiting his arrival.

It was a wonderfully clear night with the moon lighting up the pavement. Paris at moonlight was perhaps the most romantic it ever would be.

Soon he heard the words 'Adam we are ready for you on set.'

****

'Oh Tommy, I knew it! The Eiffel Tower at night is simply gorgeous! All those twinkling lights!' Sarah was more than a little excited at the vision before her.

The group had somehow stumbled their way back to find the Eiffel Tower, as the bells chimed midnight Tommy and Sarah looked up far into the starlit sky and in her ears Sarah could hear Ewan McGregor singing 'Your Song', around the corner, underneath the lit tower, Alex had just gone down on bended knee to the more than a little surprised Alice.

'My darling Alice, I love you more than words could ever say. Will you marry me?' And as he said that he produced a red velvet box from his pocket, which he had spent the whole day concealing and protecting, opening it up revealed a huge and sparkling single diamond solitaire ring.

Alice felt her cheeks redden as she became aware of an audience around her. She let him slip the ring on her finger and realised that it fitted perfectly.

'Oh Alex, I will!!' She wrapped her arms around him and they kissed each other to the applause from the onlookers.

On hearing the applause Tommy and Sarah ran round to the other side just in time to see the crowd watching two figures hugging and Sarah realised the two figures were her best friend and boyfriend.

She ran up to them and Alex turned to her as Alice could barely speak 'She said yes!'

Sarah hugged them both and Tommy joined in too 'I am so happy for you both.'

Alice couldn't stop the tears of joy from falling down her cheeks and they all held hands and made their way up the Eiffel Tower to look at Paris by night and enjoy (yet another) celebratory drink at the restaurant bar.

Sarah noticed some commotion down below and floodlights and cameras and then had to look a little harder as she made out the shape of someone that looked suspiciously like Adam in a dinner suit. People were making a fuss of him and there was one woman who was shooing away some girls nearby.

She heard a male voice say 'This is a closed set' and then the camera snapped away as Adam made brooding faces and posed, her heart leapt. She did have feelings for him.

Of all the days that he had to come to Paris why did it have to be today? She needed to avoid him at all costs. He couldn't see her with Tommy. She tugged on Tommy's sleeve 'Can we head back to the hotel now? I think we should leave these two love birds alone.' Tommy glanced over at Alex and Alice. They really were the perfect couple.

'OK let's go,' and took her hand as they made their way back down the Tower. She needed to shrug him off and as he led her one way, she turned to pull him the other. There were two exits and to avoid Adam they needed to use the other.

She dropped his hand and started walking at a fast pace ahead of him.

'Sarah wait up,' here we go again he thought, the hot and cold girl.

And just as she started to walk further away she heard another familiar voice call her name.

Sarah? We need to talk.'

She couldn't believe it, what the hell was he doing here. She turned to see David with a bunch of red roses which he obviously had bought from the street sellers and he was on bended knee.

'David, how did you know I was here?'

'Sarah look I just want to say sorry in advance but hear me out. I have been following you all over Europe. I have watched you carry on with him, I don't know who this Hooray Henry is and why the hell you are already looking at wedding venues with him,' he pointed over at Tommy who was looking on and instantly straightened up and replied.

'Now listen here, I don't know who the hell you are but just who you think you are calling me a Hooray Henry?'

David ignored him and carried on addressing Sarah, holding her hand firmly.

'I came here to say, I need you. I want you. Will you marry me?' and out came the unmistakable Tiffany blue box which he opened up to reveal what she knew as the classic Tiffany engagement ring. She gasped in admiration and then felt a pang in her heart. She had to be true to herself.

Anyone else and she probably would have said yes, this was undoubtedly the single most romantic gesture she had ever experienced but she was utterly and completely over David, so much so that it pained her to reject the most stunning and quite frankly dream ring that she had always desired.

'David, I uh, I can't. I am sorry. I meant every word I said in England. It is over, we are over.'

Adam had heard the commotion and during a brief lull in filming had heard a voice that he recognised as belonging to Sarah and that man that had serenaded her in the street.

He leapt out from behind the screen.

'Sarah?' My beautiful Sarah? What a massive surprise, what are you doing here?'

Oh no this was not what she needed, all three men in Paris at the same time. What a complete and utter mess. She felt tears falling down her cheeks. She wiped away a tear with her elbow. She had probably smeared her mascara but she didn't care.

She sighed 'Adam, it is such a long story, I don't even know where to begin. I am tired and drunk and right now I can't deal with this AT ALL.'

Tommy stepped forward and put his arm around her shoulders 'Now is probably not the time to ask but who the hell are these guys?'

'You are right Tommy, now is not the time to ask,' she spotted a taxi and stuck out her hand, it stopped and she leapt inside ordering it back to the hotel.

The three men were left standing with their mouths wide open looking in the direction of the taxi. Had she really just done that, walked away from all three of them?

Sarah couldn't believe what she had just done but she just had to get away from the absurd situation that it was. She was so relieved that the Taxi had turned up when it had and as she waltzed through the hotel lobby she felt as if she was floating on air, a weight had been lifted. They finally all knew about each other.

Tommy looked at David, David looked at Adam and Adam looked at Tommy, none of them wanted to ask the other what was going on or who they were but all said 'What the hell just happened there,' and dispersed into the crowd.

David felt like he had come off the worst, he had been publicly rejected and even after he had proposed with the long lusted after Tiffany Ring, there was no choice but to finally admit defeat. He had lost her. He hadn't done enough to convince her in those early days and now he had lost everything.

Back at the hotel Sarah collapsed into a heap on her bed and sobbed herself to sleep, just how was she going to explain all of this?

She had nightmares all through the night where all three men were surrounding her demanding answers and each yelling at her saying 'Sarah, pick me!' Her head was spinning from it all.

CHAPTER EIGHTEEN

Sarah was dreading facing Tommy this morning after the events of last night, she didn't much feel like eating but desperately needed a coffee to wake her up. She knew she couldn't avoid him for long, they had a taxi coming to pick them up and take them to the airport.

She popped on a pair of dark sunglasses, messed up her hair and made her way down the stairs hoping she had left it late enough for him to have already had his breakfast and gone to check out or at the very least that in disguise he wouldn't recognise her.

She crept into the breakfast room and glanced around to see him sat down. Damn it. She made her way to walk out again when he called out to her.

'Sarah! Morning,' oh, he seemed chirpy.

She turned back round again and styled it out.

'Ooh there you are!' Making it look like she had been looking for him all the time.

'I was wondering if you had made it down to breakfast

in time,' she lied.

'I have been here ages Sarah, you know me. I can't miss my breakfast. Not like you though to be late now is it? I bet you were trying to avoid me!'

'Anyhow, what happened to you last night, you disappeared like Cinderella. I did look around to see if you had left a glass slipper for me to hold onto but no you and the coach disappeared into thin air.'

It was just like him to make light of the crazy situation and for that this morning she was thankful. She wondered how long she could actually avoid explaining herself and decided things were better off unsaid until they returned to England.

'Can I just drink my coffee in peace?' She picked up a pain au chocolat to dunk and started scrolling through her phone.

The 'Perfect Events' Instagram account was doing exceptionally well, in just a couple of weeks they had gained thousands of followers and each picture she had uploaded had received thousands of likes and prompting people to comment. She needed to ask Alice if it was bringing any new business as a consequence. She made a mental note to update her CV with her achievements and title it 'Social Media Guru'. She may have made a mess of her love life but her work life was proving to be a success.

Tommy got a text from Alex 'Where did you two get to last night? We looked round and you had gone. Did you get lucky eh with that mix of romance and alcohol?'

He replied straightaway 'No, you won't believe it. Turns out she has two other guys on the go! Mad huh?'

Alex instantly responded 'Woah! Seriously? She is

SUCH a dark horse! Sorry mate! Do you actually know that for a fact?'

Tommy replied 'She hasn't actually said in so many words no, but it doesn't look good. To be honest I am thinking of giving up. Arabella is a right goer and at least I know she is keen.'

Sarah received a text from David 'Just to let you know. I am safely back in the UK. I am going away for a bit but you don't need to worry. I got the message loud and clear. Guess you were right. You are seeing someone else?! Or Two! I hope you can forgive me. I love you and always will. David x'

Sarah hoped this really was the last she would hear of David. She thought about texting him back to let him know she had received his message but decided against it. Where would it stop? He would probably reply and then she would feel obliged to reply and on and on it would go. She wished him no ill feelings and thought fondly of their time together, her only regret that the children had lost their daddy. She prayed that his ex-wife would let him see the kids and be a daddy to them. It was a stupid, stupid mistake that they were all paying for.

She was so relieved that it was the weekend and she could go back home and forget things for a few days. Had she not had so much tying up of loose ends to do for Tommy's party she would have booked a week off and stayed at home but as it was, she was due to be back at her desk and expected to act as if nothing had happened come Monday morning.

She texted Alice 'Thanks for coming over to Paris yesterday. It was so nice to be able to celebrate your good news!! Congratulations!! X' she didn't feel the need to bring down the mood with her news. All in good time.

The receptionist came up to their table 'Sir, Madam. Your taxi is here.'

They leapt up 'Thank you!' and got into the taxi. The driver was cute thought Sarah and then slapped her wrist. Tommy laughed. He still thought she was the cutest girl he had ever met.

No reply from Alice, she must still be sleeping, all loved up.

She stared out the window and watched the rain slapping against the glass. The weather was mirroring her mood and she just wanted to get home. Tommy sensed that she was in no mood to talk and backed off. He looked out of the other window and watched as they said goodbye to the French capital.

He certainly would not be forgetting this trip in a hurry but for now he was looking forward to Arabella's party this evening. He guessed that now Alex was practically a married man that he wouldn't be going so he messaged some other friends who agreed it would be a laugh to go along.

Sarah's phone beeped, she glanced at it and saw it was Adam. 'Can we meet up when you are back in London? Adam x'.

She replied with 'Yes I think that would be a good idea. I think there is some explaining to be done on both our parts. Sarah x'.

Maybe all was not lost with Adam.

She wondered how long this silence was going to last with Tommy and felt she should say something work related.

Now that they were on the plane, buckled up and ready to take off, she finally broke the silence.

'Tommy, I just want to run this past you as first thing Monday I am going to be booking and finalising arrangements. I think we should 100% go with the Italian Castle. It had the best feeling about it. It was practical, easy to get to and the kitchens were impressive for the caterers. Besides... what is there not to love about Rome, well apart from the drivers?!' She joked.

'I am with you on that one. Glad we are on the same page,' he smiled warmly at her. She was excellent at her job he couldn't deny it. He knew there and then that she would not be accompanying him to his party in Rome but she was quite simply the best woman to put on his party and for that he would be ever grateful. He liked to think he had found a friend for life and well you never knew what the future may hold...Never say never.

For a first client, despite the forewarning, Sarah could not have had a better one in Tommy that was for sure. Their relationship was tumultuous and up and down but she liked to think that that was because they loved each other. However, she thought the bickering was more like in a brother and sister way than lovers. She loved his smile and he did have a good heart but her heart didn't leap quite in the same way that it had done when she had first met David and even that didn't match what she felt when she would see Adam. She owed it him and herself to let him down gently. He seemed pretty keen though on her but oddly hadn't asked her about the other guys yet, perhaps he just didn't want to know.

CHAPTER NINETEEN

Sarah got home on Saturday afternoon and hugged her mum and sister and walked through to the living room to see her dad in his favourite comfy armchair. He was watching the football results, it was nice to see he still had an interest in things.

'Hi Dad,' she didn't want to make a huge fuss that he was home.

'Ah Sarah, good to see you love.'

She walked back into the kitchen where her mum and sister were sat around the table drinking tea. There was a cup of steaming tea on a coaster and she noticed her mum had dug out her favourite teenage mug from the back of the cupboard and a slice of Victoria Sponge was waiting for her. Her mum beckoned her to sit down.

'How was your work trip darling?'

She tried to put on a brave face 'Oh mum, workwise it was brilliant, but I have made such a mess of my love life. You won't believe it.' She then went on to pour out the whole sorry saga, leaving out the few passionate kisses that weren't relevant to the story and peppering it with occasional sobs and tears dripping onto the lace tablecloth.

Charlotte gave her a big hug 'My sister the temptress. Who knew?!' They both laughed and Sarah playfully punched her 'It's not funny!'

'What I want to know is how you ever thought you were going to get away with it!'

'I don't know, I guess I just thought that each of them belonged to a different part of my life and they need never meet until I was ready to make a decision or at all. Obviously I didn't intend for them to meet, ever! I really was confused you know.' She hoped they understood where she had been coming from. The last thing she wanted was her mum to think that she was a tart.

'Darling, we have all been there,' her mum whispered. Sarah and Charlotte looked at her in surprise.

She carried on whispering 'Yes, I know what you are thinking, little old mum in news shocker. Don't tell your father but when we were first dating there was sort of another man on the scene. Nothing happened mind, we didn't get up to all sorts in those days not like you kids today. So your dad was courting me and this other guy had made it clear he was also very interested. He had a convertible car and yes he was a looker, as your dad was of course. However, my gut feeling told me your dad was for keeps and so I decided he was the one I should marry.'

Sarah looked kindly towards her mum, so she did know how she felt and what she had been going through.

'Oh mum! So do you ever wonder what happened to that other guy?'

'I am sure from time to time he has entered my head but

you know something? I have no regrets. None whatsoever. Your dad has made me so happy. I just don't know what I will do if anything happens to him.' tears welled up in her eyes.

Sarah and Charlotte stood up and walked over to their mum and hugged her.

'So what I am saying Sarah is that you need to go with your gut feeling. Things will always work out in the end.'

'Thanks mum,' Sarah felt reassured.

'You drink up that tea of yours and remember whenever you need a bed or to escape to the country your dad and I are always here for you.'

Her dad called out from the living room.

'Coming dad!'

'You OK dad?'

'How's my favourite girl?'

Sarah laughed 'Sssh dad, don't let Charlotte hear!'

'Too late,' Charlotte swanned into the room and plonked herself down on the couch

They all laughed and sat down to watch 'You've Been Framed'.

'I should go help mum with dinner dad, hope you are hungry it won't be long now.'

'You are a good girl Sarah' If only he knew what she had been up to, he wouldn't be saying that Sarah thought.

After dinner her mum retired early to her bed to do some knitting in peace. She had been knitting booties for a while now, they were utterly perfect but there were no babies being born anytime soon so they were just gathering up in a huge pile on top of her wardrobe.

Charlotte went out with her friends which left Sarah and her dad sitting downstairs together. Charlotte had invited Sarah along with her but she had said no because she felt like she should stay and keep her dad company. Even if he said nothing all evening just being with him helped her feel close to him.

They sat watching the TV together in silence, when the adverts came on he finally spoke.

'So what were you two talking about with your mum in there?' His head tilted towards the kitchen.

'I heard the whispering,' nothing wrong with dad's hearing Sarah thought.

She wondered whether to lie or to just tell the truth but she was making a promise to herself to just be herself from now on. No pretence, especially with family.

'Oh dad, nothing for you to worry about. Just relationship woes but nothing I can't handle.'

'I always worry about my little girl Sarah and don't you forget it. Did you mum tell you the story of how there was this other guy hanging around when we were first courting? Is that why you were whispering?'

Sarah was gobsmacked and couldn't conceal it 'Dad! You knew? But how?'

'Us men know these things, you may think we don't understand women. But we know. I knew, of course I knew. I fought for my women and well as you can see I won my girl in the end.'

'Dad!' All these years and neither of them had said a word.

'Your mum thought she chose me but we chose each other. I couldn't let her go. She was special. That guy was never going to be a gentleman and so I warned him off.'

'You never!'

'I did. I found out where he worked and told him that she was my girl and if he knew what was good for him he should stay away. He joined the navy and we never heard from him again. Your mother doesn't know this so can we keep this to ourselves, please?'

'Dad, you intervened in fate. Mum would be devastated if she knew!'

'No sweetheart. Marrying me was our fate. When you know, you know!'

This weekend had been quite a revelation when it came to her parent's marriage. Both knew something that the other thought they didn't know and had managed many years of untold happiness. Her head was getting clearer by the minute and she thought she knew exactly what she had to do.

Her dad seemed remarkably well considering his recent ordeal and her mum was a lot more relaxed and happier now her dad was back at home. Even Charlotte had made no mention of the text that she had sent in despair earlier on in the week and so when it came to leaving on Sunday evening the family practically resembled 'The Waltons'. It was all smiles and waves as Charlotte dropped her back to the station.

'See you soon Sarah, oh and Sarah. You never did say who these guys were…'

'Charlotte, there is no need to know any more than I have already told you. Honestly, when I have a boyfriend I will be sure to bring him home to meet you all.'

'Safe journey,' they air-kissed and she left with her mood infinitely uplifted and full of hope for the future.

CHAPTER TWENTY

Monday morning came and Sarah was at her desk bright and early with a sunny disposition and her computer fired up raring to go. Alice was blissfully encased in her bubble of love and completely unaware of the drama that had occurred whilst in Paris.

'Good morning Sarah!'

'Morning Alice!'

'Coffee?'

'Ah don't worry. I'll get it. Latte?'

'Yes please.'

'Can we have a catch up meeting 10am?'

'No probs.'

Sarah called the Italian number in her diary and Giovanni answered the phone.

'Giovanni? It's Sarah, Sarah Dawes from Perfect Events. I am just calling to let you know that you will be pleased to hear that we have decided we would love to hire your castle for Mr Fawsett's party.'

'Yes? I am delighted. I look forward to welcoming you back to Rome. Thank you very much Sarah.'

'No problem, see you soon.'

She emailed Frau Jung and Monsieur Chevalier to let them know that she wouldn't be using their properties and thanked them for their time and hospitality.

She then called up all of the suppliers and confirmed date, time and location and to her delight they were all raring to go.

She had one last thing to sort out and that was the music but she had been assured by a specialist music agency that it would never be a problem to find a decent band at short notice, there were hundreds knocking about just waiting for their big break.

One final thing to spend time with Tommy for.

Spreadsheet updated and final notes made, Sarah was satisfied plans were pretty much all in place.

She entered the meeting room for her catch up meeting with Alice.

Alice's ring kept glistening as it caught the light. Sarah felt a pang of jealousy and remembered the beautiful ring that had been waiting for her had she had said yes to David. She knew it was the right decision but oh that ring!

'So first things first. I just wanted to say it was so lovely sharing with you, my best friend, what I didn't know was going to be my special day. We should hang out more often so you can get to know Alex really well. He is a great guy.'

'Yes he seems it. You never did say how you met and what a wonderful coincidence that he is Tommy's best friend!'

'Oh that story is for another time,' Alice moved on before Sarah asked any more awkward questions.

'Soooo next I just wanted to say I am loving the effort you have been making on our social media sites. You have really engaged the audience and I have to say our business enquiries are going through the roof. Our sales projections are having to be redone and I think that if we continue like this we are going to be expanding next year, moving to bigger offices AND I will be looking at taking on more staff to handle admin etc. So thank you, I really, really appreciate it. I don't want to get your hopes up but I have major plans for you and I, a promotion may very well on the line…'

'And finally, the floor is all yours dazzle me with the party plans.'

Sarah ran through the plans, detailing hour by hour, who needed to be where and what was being done by whom. Alice smiled 'Sounds like you have it covered. Good job Sarah'.

'Are you free for lunch? Let's celebrate!'

Alice was in a good mood, Sarah was in a good mood and the staff at the Tapas Bar were in a jubilant mood too. They ate a mini Spanish feast and drank Red Wine. A bit presumptuous for a Monday but what the hell, life was pretty damn great for Perfect Events and its owner.

Sarah rang Tommy.

'Hi Tommy, How are you?'

'Ah hey Sarah, how are the plans coming along?' He

kept it cool and professional.

Sarah was a little taken aback by the change in Tommy but it was just what she wanted too. Neither had broached the subject of the last night in Paris and she wasn't about to bring it up now.

'Excellent actually. We are all good to go. There is just one thing... The matter of sorting a band out. I thought we could have an iPod dock and play music from a playlist but this is obviously when the band takes their breaks. So I am wondering how you feel about accompanying me for a bit of research. I have a couple of bands lined up who I know are playing this weekend. I have checked and right now they are available for the required date. It will mean spending Friday and Saturday with me though?' She was apprehensive. Tommy hadn't been in touch since they had arrived back and now he was being cool towards her.

'Yeah sure!'

Sarah sighed with relief, this might be the last jigsaw piece in the puzzle but actually the music was a huge deal and she didn't fancy making the decision or indeed going to see any band on her own.

'OK brilliant, I shall be in touch later this week with more details. Speak to you soon.'

And that was it. For the rest of the day she tidied up some loose ends, kept in touch with their social media feeds, fielded new business enquiries and then went home to her warm flat. After the crazy European trip it was nice to be back to a semblance of normality. She opened a pack of plain salted crisps and munched through them whilst catching up on the soaps.

A text came through, it was from Adam. Her heart lurched in anticipation.

'Hey Sarah. I guess you are back now. How about that date? Adam x'

Why was he being so nice, what on earth did he think of her.

'Thursday?' She suggested as she replied back.

'Hi Adam, how are you? Would have been nice ;-)'

'Sorry, Hi Adam. How are you? Nice to hear from you. Thursday any good for you? Is that better?? Sarah x' She laughed out loud.

'Much better. Adam x'

'Well...? You never said if you could make it'

'Sure can. Adam x'

'Good. Sarah x'

'This could go on all night so I bid you a good evening. Adam x'

Sarah smiled. She was wishing it would. She fell asleep on the sofa and dreamt of her date with Adam. He was such a good kisser!

On Thursday morning she was having a shower when her mobile started ringing. She grabbed a towel and dripped all over the bathroom floor as she leapt over to her bathroom cabinet to answer it.

'Hey Sarah, I am really sorry. I am afraid I can't make it this evening. Something has come up. I would have texted but thought it better to call. Anyway can we rearrange?'

'Hi Adam. That is a shame,' she was sad, maybe he had changed his mind about the date.

'Are you sure you want to? I mean if you don't want to just tell me outright. I am not up for playing any games,' he thought that comment was a bit rich considering it was her that appeared to be stringing along three guys but he let it go for now, she did sound genuinely upset that he couldn't make it though.

'Woah steady on, yes of course! I have to work. It's a major casting that I can't get out of. I wish it wasn't so but it just is. Are you free Sunday?'

'Sunday it is. I have to go.' she had a strict time schedule in the mornings that she rarely deviated from and she could feel the clock was ticking, any longer spent on this call and she was going to be late for work.

As it happened the Northern Line was running with major delays so she was late regardless. Alice was pretty laidback about it. She didn't even ask Sarah to make the time up.

Friday came and she had arranged to meet Tommy outside The Dog and Duck. It was a hip pub whose locals were minor television celebrities and they were there to see a hot new up and coming rock band who were fast making a name for themselves.

She had pulled out the most rock chick clothes she could muster from the back of her wardrobe. She was wearing skinny black jeans suitably ripped in strategic places, a loose fitting black t-shirt with logo and pointy studded heels. As it was a bit nippy out she had popped on a black blazer over the top. She had opted for loads of black kohl around her eyes and a nice bright red lippie. She hoped Tommy appreciated the effort she had gone to in an effort to fit in.

She had phoned ahead and reserved a table, a little trick

she had learnt whilst the World Cup was on. Even so however she was running a little late and found the pub heaving. She was barely able to make her way through the front door but a little elbow shoving and sweet glances later allowed her to squeeze inside. She looked around but couldn't see Tommy and had no idea who the staff were as everyone was dressed casually. She went to the side of the bar and waited for a member of the team to come towards her to mention that she had a reservation. Thankfully they seemed to know what she was talking about and led her to a table near the front of the makeshift stage where some people were already sat, if this was her table this was going to be awkward. The man pointed at a little sign and they got up and slunk away in annoyance and it was then that she saw the handwritten card with Reserved for VIP on it. Well she wasn't about to correct them.

She ordered a drink and made herself comfortable, still no sign of Tommy. Was he going to show? Being stood up was becoming a bit of a habit for her. Then she felt a familiar hand on her shoulder.

'Hey, Sorry I am late! This place is manic,' pint in hand he sat down and gave that grin of his that she so loved. Ever cheeky Tommy.

The rock band were tremendous, really knowing how to work the crowd into a rowdy stupor. The crowd were lapping it up and the pub was well quite literally rocking. She felt the foundations shaking. Tommy had long since leapt up from his seat and had joined in with the head banging. This was a good sign thought Sarah. Tommy adored the band and although they were doing their own material they had indicated that they would be willing to do cover songs if requested. She had actually listened to their demo CD which featured a medley of well-known rock songs. Rock music wasn't really Sarah's thing but she knew a good band when she heard it.

The music stopped and the lights went on, the crowd had started going crazy 'More, more, more,' they chanted.

'Shhhh,' the lead singer pleaded for silence.

'Ladies and Gentleman you have been a fucking amazing crowd, I am afraid this is going to be our final song of the night. Goodnight.'

The crowd groaned and Tommy joined Sarah once more.

The lights went back down and the electric guitars started up again. The lead singer looked right at Sarah and winked at her sending electricity right down her spine.

And then he started singing and the crowd went wild and joined in.

They were playing Alice Cooper's 'Poison'. She wondered if she was imagining it but she was sure the singer was directing the words at her. He didn't seem to have eyes for anyone else. He broke his gaze to start bouncing around the stage and she joined in yelling the chorus.

This was so much fun, rocking on a Friday night. Tommy was leaping about mirroring the band and then caught up with it all he came up to her and planted a kiss on her lips which took her by such surprise that she found herself kissing him back.

The lead singer jumped off of the stage and shoved him out of the way.

'Hey man, she's with me!' He stood there with his arm around her and sweat dripping down his tanned face. He was really rather handsome with long dark hair and piercing green eyes. She might have been tempted for an instant to agree with him but then imagined how many girls he had probably slept with and was put off.

Tommy shoved him back 'Don't you 'Hey Man' me,' he mimicked the singer. 'You want to mind what you are saying and who to! We were about to hire you for our event but you have just blown it!'

The singer sneered at Tommy. 'We don't need your stupid gig man,' yikes, she looked for the nearest exit. Things could get nasty.

'Tommy leave it!' She pleaded, yet another crazy night in Sarah's life. Still she wouldn't want a dull life she reflected. She grabbed Tommy's arm and dragged him out.

'It's not worth it.' he knew she was right, he wasn't really a fighter. Truth be known he had been the kind of boy at school who had ran the other way if a rugby ball started heading in his direction.

'It was going so well as well. I wanted them to perform in Italy but not after that,' he reasoned. He paused for a moment and then said 'It's your fault you know.'

'Mine, how?' How had he come to this conclusion she demanded to know.

He grinned 'For being so damn hot!' She punched him playfully.

'Come on. I'll see you home.'

They stood at her doorway and he held her close 'Same again tomorrow?'

'I hope not! I do not want a repeat of tonight! Music was good though. Don't worry, this other band are supposed to be just as good.'

'Until tomorrow,' he air kissed her and skipped down the road.

Saturday went by in a haze and evening came – once again Sarah had tried to perfect her rock chic style. This time she opted for some wet look skin tight leather leggings, a ripped white t-shirt with a huge chunky black statement necklace round her neck and ankle boot heels. Her hair was poker straight and her eyes were surrounded by black eye shadow and lashings of Benefit's top selling (so the sales assistant or benebabe as they liked to be known had said) 'They're Real' Black Mascara for a fake lash look and her favourite nude lipstick. Just as she was leaving she threw on a short fake fur jacket.

She had also booked a table at this venue, this was yet another trendy pub and there were rumours that an 'A' list celeb was due to make a visit.

This time they planned to meet outside the pub and go in together, as they got there earlier than they had planned it gave them plenty of time to line up the drinks and have a chat.

'Oo ee,' Sarah wasn't entirely what sound had just come out of Tommy's mouth but he quickly followed it up with 'Very Kate Moss!' He murmured in approval. It was such a shame that they were going to be just friends, she would have been quite an asset to Fawsett Hall.

The crowd were equally raucous as Friday night's crowd and Sarah was sure she spotted a few people she recognised as being at the Duck and Dog the night before. Not really that unusual if they were diehard rock fans.

This band were, as promised, just as good if not slightly better but Sarah could see that they were infinitely more professional and worked hard for their well-deserved adulation. Luckily for her the lead singer was even more gorgeous than the sneery singer from last night and although she didn't quite get the music she found herself flirting with the lead singer safely from afar, smiling and fluttering her eyelashes. Once he became aware, Sarah felt the singer really upped his game.

The evening was going so well that she was a little disappointed when the set was coming to an end.

She turned around to look at the crowd behind her and out of the corner of her eye she was sure she spotted what looked suspiciously like Jude Law slipping out of the pub. So there had been an 'A' Lister in the audience after all, the rumours had been right. She didn't recognise anyone that he left with but if this band was good enough for Jude she was sure he was going to be good enough for Tommy. Actually she should ask him if any celebrities were going to be coming to his party or was it just the cast of Made in Chelsea. She really should familiarise herself with them as she didn't want to embarrass herself by not recognising them or calling them by the wrong name.

The gorgeous singer spoke 'You have been an awesome crowd. We will be back! We love you! Last song of the night. This is for the lady in the front row,' Sarah blushed, he was referring to her! He smiled at her and winked. She could quite easily see herself as a rock groupie. She was warming to the music, the guitar riffs and the gravelly singing voices.

A member of the bar staff came over with a drink for her and indicated the giver as the lead singer. She mouthed a thank you over to him.

Tommy seemed a bit put out 'Do you ever stop sizing men up, you seem like you are always on the look for something better?' He ranted at her.

Sarah was speechless 'I am sorry, I didn't realise,' but before she could say any more the band started up with a soft rock jukebox classic – Bon Jovi's 'You Give Love A Bad Name'. Sarah loved this song, a boyfriend had dedicated it to her once when she was a teenager and it brought back loads of youthful memories of late night drunken cigarette tasting fuelled snogs. Back then she had thought that the rest of her life would never live up to that moment or her amazing teens and yet now she realised that her twenties were shaping up to be pretty cool and she was even looking forward to what her thirties still had to bring.

The crowd loved it. The singer leapt off the stage and came down to sit beside her.

'Sarah is it?' He put his hand out to greet her.

'My manager said there would be someone special in the crowd, he wasn't wrong,' he was sweet talking her and she wasn't about to stop him.

Tommy had other ideas. 'I am Tommy, it is my event,' he wanted to assert his authority as quite frankly he was putting up the cash that would be paying the singer.

The singer hi fived him 'Good to meet you man, She is one hot chick isn't she?'

Sarah was so embarrassed. Creative types were so much more relaxed than the corporate world. She attempted to bring it back to business.

'So erm we liked what you did up there. I shall be in touch with your agency on Monday morning but it's safe to say you have got the gig.'

'Cool! Cheers,' he stood up and kissed her on the cheek. She was relieved that it wasn't on the lips as she didn't want Tommy to get jealous again and have a repeat performance of last night.

Tommy accompanied her home again 'Nice work Sarah. The band are going to be awesome. So I guess this is the last I will see of you until Italy?'

'I guess so Tommy,' she was a little sad but knew sometimes good things just had to end and what was the saying… If you love someone you have to let them go.

Tommy hugged her and tilted her head up towards him. He kissed her tenderly.

'Goodbye Sarah.'

'Goodbye Tommy,' she whispered.

That night she found herself dreaming about being the rock star's girlfriend and was enjoying the experience when she woke sleepily from the dream. She had had so much fun these past two days. Carefree and single was not at all bad. She decided that being friends with Tommy was far better than being his girlfriend. He was a good person to be friends with and although they clearly fancied each other they were both grown up enough to see that it would never work long term.

Tonight was her date with Adam. She realised that they hadn't made any firm plans for the evening but she didn't want to be the one to chase him. By lunchtime she still hadn't had any word from him and she was feeling a little angry and loads of thoughts were running through her head. He didn't really want to go out with her but was a wimp who didn't know how to let her down. What was he waiting for? He obviously didn't respect her or her feelings. With her new found confidence she didn't need a man like Adam messing her around. She would call him and tell him straight.

She dialled his number and waited for him to answer. Once she heard him pick up she launched into her rant.

'Hi Adam. I think its best we don't go any further with this. I haven't heard from you, it is just five hours until we are due to meet and I am not sure we made any firm plans. I don't know where we are supposed to be meeting and to be honest I am not up for being messed about anymore, least of all by a male model who thinks all women should fall at his feet merely by him looking at them.'

'You are so damn sexy when you are angry, you know that?' She could hear the laughter in his voice.

He was not taking her seriously, god he was so cocksure since he had become such an in demand model. She had been following his rise to success through the gossip magazines so she knew that he had had plenty of interest from brands and a huge increase in his bookings.

'Are you listening to a word I am saying?'

'Chill Sarah. As it happens I was about to call you. I thought as it is Sunday and you may have been out on the tiles last night I would let you sleep in. That's all.'

'How considerate of you!' Not believing a word of it. 'You could have called me any time before now,' she retorted.

'You want to know the truth?' The words of Tom Cruise echoed in her head 'You can't handle the truth!'

'Go on then, let's hear it,' she waited for him to come up with yet more excuses.

'The truth is that I didn't want to have to let you down. Work has been crazy, sometimes things come up at the last minute and I didn't want to make a plan with you and then cancel once again. That is the god's honest truth! Nothing more sinister than that.'

Sarah felt bad, he really was a decent bloke and she was ranting down the phone at him.

'So IF you still want to go out with this David Gandy wannabe… then just say the word, because he is ready and willing to go out with you. Sad girl.'

'So where shall we go?' She gave in, she very much wanted to go out with him.

'Oh just one thing?'

'What's that?'

'Anywhere but Pizza Express!'

They both laughed.

That evening they finally headed out on their long awaited date. Adam was such a gentleman wrapping his jacket over her shoulders to keep her warm. She had wanted to show off her long legs and willowy arms and had opted to wear a thigh skimming metallic spaghetti dress and stiletto heels. She looked beautiful but it was a tad impractical when she realised just how cold the weather had dropped. She teamed it with a pink lippie and applied her rich black liner into a classic cat flick. Simple but effective.

He had whispered to her that she looked beautiful as they sat in the taxi and she nearly died when their taxi stopped at The Savoy.

'Just stopping here for a quick drink, I hope you don't mind?'

A drink at the Beaufort Bar in The Savoy, she could think of far worse places to spend a Sunday evening. He ordered an 'Ol Blue Eyes' Cocktail for himself and she chose 'The Never-ending Story' cocktail for herself. Some nibbles arrived to accompany the drinks. She was loving it. She was used to the finer things in life through David but the Savoy had been restored not so very long ago and the bar was an Art Deco triumph of rich black and gold furnishings.

'Cheers!' He touched her glass in celebration of what she had no idea but she went with it. Why not she thought. She noticed from the corner of her eye people taking photos of her and Adam. Was this was it was going to be like, dating a virtual celebrity?

'I don't want to bring it up and put this evening on a downer.'

What was he about to say? 'So don't,' she replied.

'I have to, it's been eating away at me,' at least he was being honest.

'That night in Paris, who were the other guys you were with?'

She started from the beginning, it was time for some truths. He may not like them, yes she had been dating three guys at once but it honestly wasn't as bad as it first sounded. She explained that she was completely single now and free to date whomever. She told him how she had found it hard to shake off David but that she was certain he was now completely off the scene. She even told him how she had fallen in some ways for the aristocrat whose party she was planning but that had as far as she was concerned fizzled out to nothing. She had broken all the rules about what to talk about on a first date and whilst this wasn't strictly speaking their first date it did feel like they were starting anew.

'So here we are,' she smiled at him. 'I am looking forward to dinner.'

He was relieved. Things did sound better now he had finally got the whole story directly from her. He contemplated telling her that he had been aware of the presence of David after he had followed her one day but decided against it.

They hailed a taxi and Adam asked the driver to take them to The Shard. He was pulling out all the stops this evening. He had just had his first big pay cheque and seeing as it was partly down to Sarah that he was enjoying success he felt it only fair to share the spoils with the woman of his dreams. She had featured in many of his dreams lately that he felt himself flush with excitement at the thought of them.

He guided her towards The Shangri La Hotel and led her all the way up towards level 35 where the Ting Restaurant was situated. Adam's new found influence had bagged them a window table where they took in the spectacular views across London.

'Wow!' 'I never use this word in my life but I think this warrants a tremaze!'

'Ha ha, it is a bit isn't it.'

They ordered the Scallops to start.

'These are out of this world' Sarah exclaimed, she had never tasted food this good.

For her main she chose the delicious sounding Pork Belly and Adam went for the Lamb Loin, the fusion of European food with Asian influence was sublime.

'This is the best meal I have ever had!' she declared and

it was true.

'Me too!' 'Dessert?'

'Always room for dessert, I fancy something chocolatey. Tell me they do something like that.'

'I am sure they do.'

Once the dessert menu was in her hands she glanced down the list and found her perfect dessert. It was simply labelled Chocolate. It was a chocolate ganache with candied orange and a citrus sorbet. It sounded sweet but refreshing, a bit like Adam she thought.

As they left someone had alerted the press to the fact that he had been inside and cameras were waiting to click away when he walked out.

Sarah was a little nervous, she hoped the photos did her justice. She wondered if she would be reading about herself in the papers tomorrow. She hoped not. If she had known this was going to happen she would have applied more makeup and used HD camera ready products. Damn. He could have warned her.

Adam was feeling annoyed, he had barely been tabloid fodder for two minutes and already the press were ready and waiting to bring about his downfall.

He took hold of Sarah and pushed her into the first taxi he could find and followed her inside.

'Sorry about that. I wasn't expecting it to be honest.'

He continued 'About that, I guess it's about time I thanked you. You know if it wasn't for you I would probably still be working in my recruitment job. Things went stratospheric after THAT pic and yet when it was just on the billboard it probably would have gone unnoticed.'

He then continued to explain why he had been a bit cagey about what he did for a living pre the new modelling career, he explained how he had had a few modelling jobs but thought it a bit naff to say he was a model when he had only had a few jobs and how he thought recruitment wasn't nearly half as glamorous as he thought her job was and he had just wanted to impress her.

Just then their cosy chat was interrupted by a text from Alice.

'Hey, how was your date with Adam the heartthrob?'

'Still on it!' she replied.

'I'll leave you to it….Squee! x'

He invited her back to his place for coffee and this time she didn't say no.

CHAPTER TWENTY ONE

Monday morning brought much excitement to the 'Perfect Event' office. A major celebrity's PA had been in touch and Alice had left the office abruptly to attend a meeting with them regarding a huge bash. She hadn't left any clues for Sarah only saying that until it was confirmed she didn't want to get their hopes up so Sarah was still in the dark as to who the celebrity was, but that didn't stop her imagination going wild. Was it Elton John wanting input on his White Ties and Tiaras Ball or was it Madonna, although she was not entirely sure whether she still lived in London after her split from Guy Ritchie.

She made herself a coffee and flicked through some gossip mags to see if she could glean some information from them as to who the current 'IT' crowd were.

Alice had arrived back at the office with the biggest smile on her face, it was almost as big as the one she had had when Alex had proposed to her.

'They loved us! We got the job! Shhhh We have been sworn to secrecy, it's Kate Moss's Ibizan Dream Party this Summer!'

They both danced around the room. We are going to Ibiza!

'So, you want to tell me how it went with Adam?'

They diverted their phones to answerphone and settled down for a chat.

'Oh Sarah. That is so ace.'

'I know, it is crazy but I think I have finally met THE ONE! I just have to find a way to tell Tommy but I was thinking I will tell him after the party or actually, maybe before. He wanted me to go in fancy dress but hopefully I shall let him know in no uncertain terms that that is simply NOT happening.'

They laughed together 'Suits it is,' they said in unison.

They went through Tommy's party plans for one last time before the big event.

The checklist was completed, deposits and confirmation confirmed and they were ready to fly at the end of the week.

Sarah was glad her best friend was going with her and seeing her through her first ever event, things could get ugly with Tommy when she had to turn him down and yet again she wished she had never crossed the line between client and lover but it had happened so she just had to suck it up.

Tommy had no intention of taking things further with Sarah but wanted to pull her leg so called her up to wind her up.

'Hey gorgeous! You got your costume ready?'

'Tommy, I. I erm I am sorry. About the costumes, Alice and I think that we should keep things professional from our side and wear suits. It's just so that if the suppliers have any issues they can spot us easily and quickly. So you see, it makes total sense, don't you think?'

'Relax, I wasn't really expecting you too! I was just kidding.'

'See you in Italy!'

Well he took that well she thought, now just to break off the looming relationship. To Italy it was.

CHAPTER TWENTY TWO

Alice and Sarah made their way to Italy in advance, they had gone ahead to oversee the suppliers and installers of the decorations and to ensure that all the preparations ran smooth ready for the big event.

Giovanni was on hand to greet them.

'Sarah' he said except it was spoken in his charming and smooth Italian accent and came out rather like this 'Sar rah.'

'An absolute pleasure to see you again,' he took her hand up to his lips and kissed it.

'He is smooth!' Alice whispered to Sarah egging her on.

'Isn't he just! Shame he is gay!'

'No way! He looks so much like George Clooney.'

'Yes well his looks aren't really much to my taste but it is true. I heard him on the phone to his lover. He spoke so gently it was like he was caressing the phone!' They gossiped.

Giovanni greeted the suppliers and showed them

around the place which made Sarah and Alice's job a little redundant and he was equally charming and enigmatic to them as well. The man was so kind and genuine it made Sarah almost sad she was unlikely to work with him again after this.

Sarah was left to sort out the band and she felt that familiar pang when she saw the lead singer again. He was naughty flirting with her like that, especially now that he no longer had to be so nice to her, but still she wasn't going to tell him to stop. Adam had been sent on a job for an aftershave advert to a far flung exotic location with a beautiful model and was to be gone a whole week. Since they had got together they had barely been apart and she was already missing him like crazy and a little jealous that she couldn't have gone with him, it was still early days in their relationship and she wasn't going to lie, she was concerned he may fall for his leading lady. Going to Italy was going to be a welcome distraction, she hoped she was going to be so busy she wouldn't have time to even think about him and the mischief he could get up to. It was true she wasn't entirely up for trusting him completely just yet.

Sarah wandered over to the kitchen area where she caught a glimpse of Arabella's impossibly long lean legs, the woman just oozed class and it didn't help that even though she was setting up and cooking she still felt fit to wear a pearl necklace. She slipped out as quickly as she had slipped in. She wasn't keen to make small talk with her. She didn't really have anything in common with her or knew what to say apart from 'Nice Hog' which was akin to saying 'I carried a watermelon' ie positively stupid!

Once Sarah and Alice were sure that the set up was running to schedule, they were happy to leave the suppliers to it and under the watchful gaze of Giovanni who had promised to call if any hitches occurred. Like Thomson

Reps they had made sure they were ready and waiting for the guests coming off the planes to get onto the coaches that had been generously laid on. They had even had some 'Perfect Events' personalised logo sashes made especially for the occasion to make themselves stand out from the other people waiting at arrivals.

Tommy and Alex were travelling on the last group plane due to arrive at the airport. They had spent the short flight talking about women and generally flirting with the charming hostesses, who were a little tired of their shenanigans and so had arranged for the male staff to switch areas and soon their fun was curtailed. Their chat turned back to their own relationships.

'Alex old chap, I am seriously delighted for you. Alice seems like such a lovely girl.'

'She is, she really is.'

'Shame it isn't going to work out with Sarah, just think of all the things we could have done together.'

'Yeah it is a pity, but it's just the way it is. To be honest I probably knew she wasn't for me the day I saw her looking at that famous model bloke. I am so far apart from that ideal, it wasn't going to happen.'

'Still, Arabella's party was something, wasn't it?' Alex had gone along after all.

Arabella had put on a rather riotous evening of debauchery which her upper class friends had thoroughly approved of. Tommy was also a fan but if he thought he had stood a chance with her after their last meeting she was playing hard to get. She remained rather elusive the whole night and he left without even so much as kissing her.

'Sounds like you may have a soft spot for her?'

'Well… you never know!'

'She is coming isn't she, to Italy I mean?'

'Coming, she is one of our main food suppliers. It is going to be ace. Her Hog Roast is to die for! That is NOT a euphemism!'

'I think she is already there, at least I bloody hope she is!'

Stepping off the plane they felt the warm air on their skin.

'Welcome to Rome, the city of love, breathe it in, lap it up.' Alex laughed.

'It's all right for you! Your fiancé is with you. What am I going to do?'

'You will think of something!'

They walked out with their luggage and spotted Sarah and Alice.

'Aye Aye, Ladies at 12 o'clock.'

'Steady old chap,' they joked with each other.

Alex greeted Alice with a kiss while Tommy air kissed Sarah. He was doing his utmost best to keep his hands off of her. He knew she was no longer on the market as Alice had told Alex who in turn had spilt the beans to Tommy. He didn't want his best friend to make a fool of himself and this way at his own party he may have a chance with a certain potential love interest.

On the coach Sarah and Alice felt like teachers trying to maintain control of naughty public schoolboys, who knew grown men could make so much noise but it was all in good spirits and thankfully no one was overly drunk just yet.

The venue was lit up on the outside and the marquee was put up as well as the evening was set to be warm and dry. The drinks were flowing and the serving staff were dressed up as ghoulish characters walking around keeping guests topped up with drink and canapés. The playlist was going down a storm and neither Tommy nor Sarah could wait for the band to start at 9pm. The lead singer had made it clear that his band did not do requests on the night, their playlist was carefully selected and tightly rehearsed which both of them had been happy enough to go along with.

The marquee was set up with circular tables for the sit down dinner, well in the event they changed their minds and decided that rather than have a complete sit down dinner they would have the guests line up to get a hog roast dinner and then choose a table to sit down at, far easier than having a table plan which would have caused a major headache for Tommy and was something he had been quite vocal as being keen to avoid.

Sarah and Alice kept in contact through headphones, the venue was big enough for them to require it and Giovanni was also included in the group. He was such fun and considerate. Sarah was so happy that both she and Tommy had agreed on this being the best venue, Giovanni certainly was the best man for the occasion too.

Every so often one of Tommy's friends would walk past Sarah and shout in her face 'Great party' in a wonderful cut glass accent. She was so pleased that everyone seemed to be enjoying themselves.

She noticed Alice taking a little break in the corner and using the time to get even better acquainted with Alex. She smiled and thought of her romantic night in Italy with Tommy when he had just for one night turned into a sophisticated gentleman and their time throwing coins into the Trevi Fountain.

Number one had come true – They had returned to Rome, Number two had also come true for Sarah – she did have a new romance, the one with Adam. But what about Tommy? She suddenly felt very guilty.

Tommy started tapping his glass.

'Can everyone be quiet please for just a moment?'

'Speech, Speech, Speech,' the crowd roared.

'Ssshhhh,' Alex's deep loud voice managed to rise above the crowd.

Tommy started his speech 'I just want to say a few words and then I will let you all enjoy the rest of the evening.'

'As you know last year was a bit of a shitty year for me, what with the loss of my girlfriend who at the time seemed like she was the love of my life, it hit me hard. You as my friends know, as with anything in my life the answer is always a PARTY.'

'Yes' someone in the crowd whooped.

'I had the pleasure of meeting the wonderful Alice and Sarah from 'Perfect Events' who promised to put on the best party ever for me. Advert alert – 'That is Perfect Events', stand up ladies..Make yourself known.'

Sarah and Alice stood up from the back of the marquee and blushed to great applause.

'Well I think you will agree it is rocking!'

More applause from the guests surrounded them

'For this amazing party and stunning venue we have the utterly delightful Sarah to thank, I know just how much work she has done and how much work and effort has gone into organising this evening so she deserves a massive thanks.'

'Can we please raise a glass to Sarah,' the guests all raised their glasses

'To Sarah,' they all repeated.

And then he started up again 'Sarah please come and join me here.'

Oh no what was he going to do now? For a moment there she honestly thought he was going to propose, she apprehensively walked to the front of the room to where he was and stood beside him.

Out of his pocket came a small and pretty looking box. 'Oh no he isn't! She was aghast.

'Tommy no, I don't think this is such a good idea,' she pleaded with him to stop.

Tommy ignored her protestations and continued with his speech 'Please will you accept this small gift as a token of appreciation from me to say thank you,' he paused. 'For everything.'

More rapturous applause as she accepted the gift and slunk away back to the back of the marquee to resume her duties. She couldn't explain just how relieved she was that this wasn't a proposal.

'Enjoy the drinks, enjoy the band. To partying.'

The guests all raised their glasses one final time 'To partying!'

The hog roast was going down a storm, the mini desserts were being salivated over and the evening was flowing smoothly.

Alice walked over to Sarah 'Great party Sarah, well done!'

'Thanks Alice. It is just a shame that Adam couldn't be here to join me, but I guess I am technically working.'

'The band is due to start up, take a break whenever, enjoy the band. I heard they are brilliant.'

'They are! Jude Law is a fan. I spotted him in the audience, of course he could just like the pub they were playing at,' they giggled.

Tommy made his way over to Sarah.

'Sarah will you do me the honour of having the first dance?'

'Ha ha, of course!'

He led her back to the main hall where the band had been set up.

Luckily for her the first song was a wild, get the crowd on the dance floor number so there was no need for much body to body contact.

As his friends joined him and started their head banging session she sloped away and sent a text to Adam just to remind him that she was still waiting back at home for him. Well it wasn't strictly true but she hoped that the sweet little text would make him miss her as much as she was missing him right now.

She went upstairs to the toilet and passed by a few of the bedrooms on her way, the ones she noted that they hadn't hired, and could hear voices coming out of them. She should have known a few guests would take advantage of the rooms and indulge in romantic liaisons. She smiled to herself, had she had someone special to share the evening with no doubt she would have been partaking too. She marched on towards the bathroom with the Jacuzzi bath, she was just about to open the bathroom door and enter and as she did so a vision greeted her.

There was Tommy and Arabella in the ample sized bubble bath, entwined in a passionate embrace with her long legs wrapped around his torso. They turned around, their faces like rabbits caught in headlights.

Arabella was for once speechless and buried her head in Tommy's neck and Tommy could only just get his words out 'Sarah, I. I didn't mean for you to find out like this. I am sorry.'

Sarah backed out slowly, she laughed with relief. They were so much better suited to each other than she and Tommy had ever been. 'It's ok Tommy. I have found someone too. You should lock the door though!' Reassuring him and giving him advice both at once.

And she closed the door behind her and went to find another toilet.

That Jacuzzi bath that both Tommy and Sarah had set their eyes on the first time they had visited Italy was finally being put to good use she thought. It did look extremely tempting and incredibly indulgent in its marble surroundings. Once again she lamented the fact that Adam wasn't here with her so that they could have tried it out.

Well that was it, when it came to Tommy she was off the hook, David had finally got the message and was off the scene and finally she was free to date Adam with no complications.

Just then Alice came running towards her, her face ashen white.

'There you are! I have been looking all over for you.'

'What is it, is it the party? Is there a problem?' Damn it she thought, she had taken her eyes of the ball for just a few minutes and clearly a disaster had occurred but what on earth could it be. The revellers seemed to be oblivious to anything, was it an industrial accident in the kitchens?

'I think you'd better sit down Sarah,' Alice took Sarah's hand and led her to a chair.

Oh no, a million thoughts starting running through her mind. Was it her dad? Had he taken a turn for the worse and on it went until Alice swiftly put her out of her misery.

'Sarah. I am so sorry. It's David. He was knocked over whilst crossing the road last night. He died at the scene. I am sorry darling,' she hugged her tight.

Sarah felt numb, thank goodness Alice had had the foresight to sit her down. God this was awful. Just moments before she had been thinking with relief that David had got the message and was going to leave her alone and now it was final. There was no going back now if she had had second thoughts about Adam. She would never see him again. How on earth must his poor family be feeling?

'But how do you know, who told you?' She was confused.

'His boss Dan, we had been in contact after the whole stalking incident. He thought you would want to know. He had tried to contact you direct but didn't have your new number.'

Sarah felt sick to the stomach. This had been such a shock and yet she wanted to continue with the job in hand, Alice seemed to read her thoughts.

'Are you ok? I mean obviously you are not. You can go home now if you want?'

'No, it's ok. What would I do then? I would only be alone. I would rather be here with you. Busy. I will be ok, honest.'

CHAPTER TWENTY THREE

Police were still looking for the hit and run driver who had struck David that fateful evening. It had warranted a brief appeal on the local television evening news and a small reward had been put up by his family, although a few people had rung in that evening with some potentially interesting information the leads had led to nowhere.

Sarah had gone to David's funeral. She had wanted the chance to say goodbye. She had sat and watched from the back of the Church as the service went ahead. She saw his children bravely speak about their wonderful dad and his brother spoke about all the things that David had achieved in his life that had been cruelly cut so short. Then David's wife stood up to speak with a heartfelt speech that moved everyone to tears, she said that although they had had their fair share of problems they had been recently reconciled, reaffirming their love for each other and were due to have renewed their vows in this very Church. She watched as her hands shook with distress and it was then that she saw it sparkling under the lights, on her finger sat the unmistakeable Tiffany Ring that David had proposed to her with. At least it had gone to a good home and David's wife would cherish it forever.

She waited for the mourners to leave and then she went up to the grave alone unseen. She rested a single red rose down and whispered.

'Goodbye David.'

Another chapter in her life had closed.

****

Sarah had been upfront with Adam for her need for time to mourn David. Adam to his credit had been very understanding and had given her the space she had craved. Alice too had said she could have the week off if she felt she needed it and she had gladly taken her up on the offer.

Sarah headed home and spent a much needed week of relaxation with her family. Her dad was well enough to be able to go out for Country walks with her and her mum had bounced back to her old cheery self. Sarah watched her mum and dad together and only hoped that she could emulate their happiness in her relationship with Adam. Charlotte had even stayed home come evening time and introduced Sarah to her new partner Philip. He seemed really nice and her mum had mentioned that they had even allowed him to stay over on the odd occasion.

Refreshed, she returned to London. She got a surprise when she returned to her flat and turned the key. A huge bunch of her favourite flowers were sat in a vase in the middle of her coffee table. Beside it someone had placed a couple of magazines and a big bottle of Jo Malone's Lime Basil and Mandarin Bath Oil. This had to be the work of Adam. She opened her fridge and found a fresh carton of milk. No doubt about it, this man was for keeps.

She called him.

'Thank you Adam.'

'No worries. I hope you are ok and enjoy your pamper afternoon at home. Would you like me to come round later?'

'That would be lovely.'

They spent the evening together watching a romantic comedy and he had brought round some food saying that he didn't think she would be in the mood for cooking for which she was grateful. He stayed overnight using the excuse that she probably didn't want to be alone. 'You are funny Adam!'

'Who me?' He gave her a playful tickle.

In the morning she was greeted with the scent of coffee brewing in the cafetiere.

'I don't have anything to do today, let me accompany you to your office.'

'Ooh I better not get used to this, what will happen when you are away for work? What will I do then?'

'Then my dear, I am afraid you are on your own!'

'Charming.'

They squashed together onto the packed tube and watched the miserable faces of their fellow commuters going about their business. If only she could share the happiness she was now feeling, maybe they too would be smiling.

The commute was over all too soon and they found themselves standing outside the 'Perfect Events' office.

'Well I guess this is you!'

'Thanks Adam, you didn't have to you know. I have been perfectly capable of seeing myself to work these past few months.'

'I know, I wanted to.'

He kissed her tenderly and as she turned to go inside affectionately patted her bottom.

'Knock 'em dead!'

Work had been chaotic since the society pages had been filled with images of Tommy's Italian extravaganza. The whole thing had been a success from start to finish and had, as predicted, put 'Perfect Events' on the world map. Tommy and Arabella's relationship had been revealed to the world that night and the gossip columns had been going wild with speculation as to their future plans. They really were perfectly suited and an engagement announcement was imminent. Tommy's family had happily passed over the running of Fawsett Hall to Tommy now he was settling down with the impressible and capable hands of Arabella. Arabella being the formidable businesswoman that she was, was sure to make the running of Fawsett Hall and its newly appointed status as a National Trust Venue a massive success.

As a result of the media coverage the amount of enquiries meant that Alice could be a lot choosier about which clients to take on and she upped their prices accordingly for their expertise. Alice had in Sarah's absence already had to take on a Junior to log all enquiries and carry out general admin work but was well aware that they needed at least another member of staff to take on more of the workload, especially as she was going to be promoting Sarah to partner.

Alice had already started to make enquiries into renting

new premises and her accountant was delighted with the way the figures were imploding and beating projections on almost a monthly basis.

It was funny how things work out thought Alice, not so long ago, although she hadn't admitted it to Sarah, she was thinking of closing 'Perfect Events' up to go travelling because it wasn't quite working out how she had imagined. Finding new business was proving to be tougher than she had expected and at the time it seemed event planners were not in huge demand. It was only the chance meeting with Alex that fateful girl's night out that had led her to Tommy who had catapulted her business to these extraordinary new levels. In employing Sarah (at Tommy's request) they had found a natural, born organiser and the rest was as they say history.

A phone call came in from Adam's Manager. Alice took the call.

'Am I speaking to Alice at 'Perfect Events'? This is Katie DeVere, Adam Coult's manager. I have been contacted by a major morning television programme's research team regarding their Human Interest story section. They absolutely love the fact that Adam has been effectively created as a superstar model from one image placed on social media by your company. They think it would definitely be something that their viewers would be interested in. I was wondering if we could hold a joint interview with the person who put this image up on your Instagram site. Adam has told me that it is someone called 'Sarah' is it possible to speak to her?'

'This is Alice. I am afraid Sarah is not in the office at the moment but I will be sure to pass on the message when she gets in. We will be in touch.'

Alice wasn't about to tell Katie that Adam and Sarah

were actually now in a relationship. It wasn't her place to say.

She put the phone down and as she did so Sarah walked into the office. She spoke excitedly.

'I have had a call from someone called Katie DeVere, she is Adam's manager apparently. She wants you and him to go on a morning TV programme. You won't believe it but they think their viewers would be interested in how you put up his image on our company Instagram account by accident and how it led to him becoming a major International Model.'

Sarah was stunned.

So that was how two days later Sarah found herself sat beside Adam on a sofa being interviewed for daytime TV.

'Meet Adam and Sarah, you may recognise Adam as the top male model who has burst onto the advertising scene, seemingly overnight. Sarah, who is sat next to him is responsible for his success in this very modern tale of how Social Media made him a star and how love has blossomed as a result.'

'Welcome both of you, Sarah can you tell us the story of how Adam's image ended up appearing on your company's Instagram account and what happened next?'

'Yes, well actually you are not going to believe this but to be perfectly honest it was completely unintentional and in error. The picture I took that day was never intended for publication in that way. It was for my eyes only but once it was done as with most things, it couldn't be undone.'

CHAPTER TWENTY FOUR

A year later the newly engaged Sarah and Adam were happily standing watching as Tommy and Arabella were taking their vows of marriage in St Pauls Cathedral. Alice was standing alongside them whilst Alex, as Tommy's best man, was next to Tommy.

Sarah smiled as she recalled that Tommy's happiness was probably all down to her too, after all if she hadn't shortlisted Arabella's company as one of the Hog Roast suppliers they would probably never have met.

This time however they were all together as guests at the Society wedding of the year. Arabella had apologised for not handing over the planning of the wedding to 'Perfect Events' but had stated that she would be far happier for them to attend the wedding as her guests and not have to worry about a thing whilst sharing their special day. The reception was held in Fawsett Hall and the guests were treated to a no expenses spared five course sit down meal and a midnight Hog Roast supplied by Arabella's company of course.

Alex and Alice had yet to tie the knot due to her

mountainous workload but had made plans to slip away abroad for an intimate wedding witnessed by their nearest and dearest later in the year.

The End

ABOUT THE AUTHOR

Bettina Hunt lives with her husband and two young children in Essex. She is an avid reader and has been so ever since she was first taught to read by nuns at her nursery school.

With a voracious appetite for the written word, she would walk out of the library reading a book and have finished it by the time she arrived home.

In Secondary School she was known as the 10/10 girl for the marks she was given for her imaginative stories in English class. Starting off by sharing poems and short stories on her website www.beautyswot.com to great response, she finally put pen to paper to fulfil a lifelong dream.

'A Tempting Trio' is her debut novel, but she is busy writing books two and three.

Printed in Great Britain
by Amazon